E

HERITAGE OF NURSE O'HARA

HERITAGE OF NURSE O'HARA

Colleen L. Reece

Thorndike Press • Chivers Press
Thorndike, Maine   Bath, England

This Large Print edition is published by Thorndike Press, USA and by Chivers Press, England.

Published in 1999 in the U.S. by arrangement with Colleen Reece.

Published in 1999 in the U.K. by arrangement with the author.

U.S. Hardcover 0-7862-2033-3 (Candlelight Series Edition)
U.K. Hardcover 0-7540-3868-8 (Chivers Large Print)

The text of this Large Print edition is unabridged.
Other aspects of the book may vary from the original edition.

Set in 16 pt. Plantin by Al Chase.

Printed in the United States on permanent paper.

British Library Cataloguing in Publication Data available

Library of Congress Cataloging in Publication Data

Reece, Colleen L.
     Heritage of Nurse O'Hara / Colleen L. Reece.
         p.   cm.
     ISBN 0-7862-2033-3 (lg. print : hc : alk. paper)
     1. Large type books.   I. Title.
[PS3568.E3646H47 1999]
813'.54—dc21   99-27127

HERITAGE OF NURSE O'HARA

Chapter 1

The closely written pages of her father's letter cascaded through Laurel O'Hara's nerveless fingers and drifted to the rich crimson rug. Unheeding, she sat huddled in the big white chair by the window, motionless as the original Ice Maiden. A parting ray of sunlight rested lightly on the glistening dark hair and cornflower blue eyes but failed to restore the usual dusky rose that had fled from her cheeks as she unbelievingly read the letter. At last, as though discouraged, the setting sun covered its face behind a low rise, and she was alone.

Hours passed. Still Laurel remained frozen by the window, little seeing the lights that sprang on as first dusk, then complete darkness fell. It wasn't until the clock struck ten that her inborn sense of duty roused her. I can't work tonight, she thought in panic, I must think. Rapidly crossing to the telephone she switched on the table lamp and dialed Mountainside, the private hospital just outside Phoenix where she was due on night shift at eleven. Mrs. Murray, Head R.N. on Ward 4, answered.

"I know it's short notice," Laurel apologized, breathless, "but can you possibly get another nurse to work for me tonight?" She hesitated a moment, then forced the words through her tightening throat.

"Something unexpected has come up."

It was an unusual request. In the year Laurel had worked at Mountainside, it was the first time she had asked for a substitute. She could hear Mrs. Murray clicking the call board even as she answered.

"Laurel, what's wrong? You sound so strange. Are you ill?"

The stricken girl swallowed back tears at the concern in her supervisor's voice.

"I just don't feel very well, Mrs. Murray."

There was silence again for a moment, then the head nurse said, "All right, Laurel. Don't worry about tonight. Beth can help out. Take care of yourself and let me know tomorrow if you'll be in."

"Thank you, Mrs. Murray." She slowly cradled the phone and sank back in her chair. I can't sleep, she decided. Not until I've thought this all out. Determinedly she pulled the heavy crimson drapes that matched the rug, touched a match to the well-laid fire, and snapped off the table lamp, then curled up on the white couch facing the fire. Usually the pattern of the dancing flames on the soft cream walls

8

brought a sense of peace, but not tonight. Her mind was too full of her father's letter.

Dad! Even after these weeks without him sometimes her loneliness was almost unbearable. They had been so close. Laurel's mother had died in childbirth and big red-headed Mike O'Hara had been both father and mother to her, as well as Chief Surgeon at Desert General.

Laurel remembered when she was a child once she had asked, "Was my mama beautiful? Do I look like her? Why did she have to die when I was born? You're a good doctor, Daddy. Why didn't you make her get well?"

A look of pain crossed his face. "Yes, Laurel, she was beautiful. You have my blue eyes, but her dark hair and complexion. She was very beautiful, Laurel, but I couldn't save her." Laurel never asked again. Even then she seemed to realize how deeply hurt her father was. It somehow explained why there were no pictures of Laurel's mother, and she grew up loving her father even more because there were only the two of them.

Dr. O'Hara's pride when she told him she had decided to enter nursing school was beyond bounds. He had never pushed her, believing it best for her to stand alone in her choice of a career, but nursing was all she wanted. When she graduated head of her class, he bought her a white Mustang with red interior, to "match your coloring," he said.

He agreed when she told him wistfully, "I'd like to work in 'your' hospital, Dad, but I don't want the name of 'teacher's pet.' I've applied at Mountainside." A few weeks later she was accepted and had been on the Children's Ward nearly a year. Since his death three months ago she had asked for night shift — it helped cut down the lonely hours.

The only thing they had disagreed on was Laurel's growing attraction for young Dr. Grant Carson, resident doctor at Mountainside.

"I know you're old enough to pick for yourself, honey," he told her, "but he just isn't good enough for you."

Laurel laughed and demanded, "Would anyone be, in your opinion?"

"Well . . . no," he admitted with a sheepish grin, and Laurel continued to date the handsome, dark-eyed doctor whenever they both were free.

A fresh pang shot through her. It still seemed unreal. To all appearances Dr. O'Hara was in perfect health, then one eventful day following a successful operation, he collapsed in the scrub room. It was the old story of long hours and not enough rest. Now, in a matter of days, his heart would refuse to function entirely.

"Do something!" Laurel stormed, unable to accept what was happening, but the cardiac specialist only shook his head.

"I'm sorry, Laurel. It's too late for that now."

Two weeks later Dr. O'Hara died, and Laurel was alone as never before in her life. Her world turned black, and if it hadn't been for the understanding of Grant Carson, she didn't think she could have pulled through those first few weeks.

The cardiac man had given her a letter after the funeral. "He said not to read it for a while, wait until you've been able to accept things better," he told her. Listlessly Laurel nodded. The last thing she could bear would be a letter from her father, written under such circumstances.

She carefully put it away in her jewel case until the time seemed right. It would be a talisman, something to look forward to, when she was ready.

Today had seemed to be that time. She arrived home from work about eight A.M., showered in the sunny yellow and orange bathroom off her bedroom and slept until almost five. When she awakened she felt alive again. The pain was still there, but things were more in perspective. For the first time since her father's death she could look around her bedroom with quiet enjoyment. Dr. O'Hara had had it redecorated for her while she was on assignment for a few weeks at the State Mental Hospital during her senior year of nursing school. A feeling of loving warmth spread through her as she glanced around the big room. Off-white walls, sheer turquoise curtains with lime and turquoise drapes, a turquoise rug and spread, a great wardrobe for her clothes. All bright colors, those she loved best.

She lay perfectly still in enjoyment of the freedom from worry, noticing the singing of a bird outside her window, the stealthy beam of late-afternoon sunlight trying to filter through the curtains.

Suddenly there was an urgency within her to read her father's last message. Hurrying to her jewel case, she took out the thick envelope with her name in the beloved handwriting. Only stopping to snatch up a quilted turquoise robe and matching slippers, she padded through the heavily piled living-room rug to her favorite chair by the window. Her fingers trembled, but at last she had the envelope open. Biting back the

12

quick rush of tears that rose within her she started to read.

Dear Laurel,

Where do I begin? What can I say to make things a little easier for you? How can I tell you that everything I've done has been because of the love of a father, even though I may have been wrong?

Laurel, try not to let my going get you down too much in spite of the loneliness. You know I've always had a great curiosity about death. I've seen so many struggle until near the end, then suddenly be filled with peace and calm. Sometimes there is a brightening of the eyes, as though before leaving this world they've caught a glimpse of something better. Often it's merely a smile, or a look. Yet I know whatever is out there has no place in it for dread or fear. Remember how you cried as a child when the fall flowers died and the bulbs turned brown? We planted them again, and the spring sun and rain brought them to a new life, even more beautiful than before. That's what I know is happening to me.

It is impossible to be in our profession and not believe in that power higher than ourselves. So many times I've seen miracles and felt a presence while in surgery. Now I'll be able to understand it. I don't want to preach, neither do I want you to grieve needlessly. My only regret is leaving you behind.

Laurel, I must break a promise I made to myself over twenty years ago. I realize now that in my own pain and bitterness I have deprived you of knowledge of yourself and your rich and proud heritage. I hope you will understand why I've kept silent all this time when you hear the whole story, part of which I only learned this week.

Twenty-five years ago when I graduated from medical school it was with high hopes of changing the world. I turned my back on more tempting offers and searched out a tiny spot where medical help was desperately needed. It was Vista d'Oro, "View of Gold," a village on the northern Arizona Navajo Indian Reservation. There I planned, dreamed, and begged sponsors until I could set up a small clinic, the only one for a hundred miles.

My dream was to show the people a better way of life than the parched corn they were able to raise in the hard red earth without much water. The village

14

was too far off the beaten path to attract tourists. The people had a few sheep, a hard life. Many of them were dying of malnutrition.

You must remember, Laurel, things were very different then. It was before Glen Canyon Dam and the influx of various businesses. It took a long time for the people to accept me and that I really cared about them. It took even longer for them to trust me enough to accept the help the clinic could give.

One of the first to catch part of my dream was the chief of the tribe. He allowed his daughter, Cloudy Willow, to come to the clinic, learn of nutrition, prenatal and baby care, and the hundred and one other ways she could teach her people.

As her knowledge grew, so did my respect and admiration. Here was a young woman with only a limited education, yet she was gifted in understanding and comprehended things often better than I could with all my schooling! I realized I had fallen very deeply in love with her. I was stunned! In all my planning, there had been no provision made for love.

That afternoon I climbed the mesa above town and sat in the shade of a gnarled pinyon tree. Behind me lay Echo Cliffs, and further on, the great Grand Canyon. Before me was the sloping country, broken by strange rock formations that led to the Painted Desert. I would stay there until I knew myself. Through the long drowsy hours I searched my very soul, and with sunset the answer came.

The final rays of the sun on the sagebrush and low rises softened the bare land, showering it with a golden light. I was seeing for the first time why the early Spaniards who traveled through named it Vista d'Oro, "View of Gold." It was a shimmer of light and color, liquid and flowing, shadows and shade, in every shade of gold from palest cream to rich topaz.

In the midst stood the white clinic, a little distance from the simple homes and hogans of the people. My clinic, my village. My heart swelled within me as I added to myself, *and my people.*

I knew I would be entirely content to spend the rest of my life here. My decision was made, I was free to seek Cloudy Willow's love. I would never take her where she might be despised because of her race, as so many others had who had married

16

and gone to the cities. We would stay here in the hard yet beautiful land.

Did she care? I thought so. Many times in the clinic I had felt her eyes on me.

It took a lot of persuasion, Laurel, to win Cloudy Willow. Her father considered a long time before he came to me, holding out his hand in friendship and saying, "Son." Cloudy Willow was an only child, and her parents worshipped her, yet I think they both knew I would make her happy.

I can never put into words what our marriage was like. It was a perfect mating, a blending of lives and personalities until we became like two blades creating one pair of scissors. It broke down barriers between her people and the clinic. More and more of them sought help, which both of us could give now. I had trained Cloudy Willow as a surgical nurse and helper — no one has ever been better. She anticipated my every need and lives were saved when I couldn't have done it alone. She offered prayers to the Great Spirit before and after each case, and more and more I realized her Great Spirit and the God of the white people are one.

She longed for children. There was nothing physically wrong, yet it was over three years before babies came. I laughed and told her that she had made her mother Many Tears wait long for her, now her child was doing the same!

If Cloudy Willow was beautiful before pregnancy, she was stunning during it. Her happiness was contagious; the whole community rejoiced. It would be the only grandchild of their chief, and they were pleased.

As the time drew near, I became alarmed. She seemed much further along than she should be, and a trace of toxemic poison was beginning to show.

"Next week I'm taking you to Flagstaff," I told her. "I can't give you all the care you need."

Although she nodded I could see the disappointment in her eyes. She wanted to have her baby right here at the clinic.

"Next time," I teased, and her face broke into a smile again.

That night I was working late at the clinic finishing reports when someone pounded at the door.

"Come quick!" The panting boy stopped for breath. "My father — his horse fell on him." The boy had run for hours to get to the clinic for help.

How could I go? What if something

18

happened to Cloudy Willow? But if I didn't . . .

"I'll be all right," Cloudy Willow assured me. She was looking better and surely I could be back soon.

With my young guide bracing himself, I drove the jeep across the moonlit desert, concerned over what lay ahead, haunted by what lay behind.

Big Sam was badly hurt, too badly to stand the long hours in the jeep back to the clinic. There was a deserted hogan I knew of a little ways away. If we could get him there, maybe he had a chance.

Testing the syringe, I gave him an injection of painkiller, and finally we got him to the hogan. There was much to do, a bone to set, cuts and scrapes to attend to and bandage. Then all we could do was wait, and hope.

The second day he was improved enough for the fever to break, and late that afternoon we pulled into Vista d'Oro. A strange quietness hung in the air. Not a child was on the street, no dogs barked in welcome. We got Big Sam bedded down in the clinic and I hurried home. A group of Navajos stood silently in the yard.

Fear clutched me as I opened the front door.

"Cloudy Willow!" There was no answer so I pushed on into the bedroom. She was there, pale and still, lying on the bed, with a slight smile. She was as beautiful in death as she had been in life. From behind me came a cry as Many Tears stepped to the bedside, a blanketed bundle in her arms. Then I understood.

"When did it happen?" I asked hoarsely.

"Yesterday. She got sick the night you left. Then yesterday the baby came, and . . ." She shrugged helplessly.

Accusingly I turned on her. "Why didn't you take her to the hospital in Flagstaff like I planned? Your son has driven our car many times. The keys were here, there was time. Why didn't you take her?"

Not a muscle of her face moved.

"Cloudy Willow's baby should be born here. I took care of her."

I stared uncomprehendingly, then the full impact of her words struck me. My house of cards lay in bits at my feet. All this time, the work I had done was useless. The suspicion and prejudice, and yes, superstition, had been stronger than my teachings. I had been accepted because I was one of them, but not the white man's ways, the hospital that could have saved my wife.

I stumbled to a chair by the bedside. Cloudy Willow was gone! A tearing sob rose within me as I reached for the little brown hand with my wedding ring.

Many Tears eyes glistened with sympathy as she laid the bundle in my arms.

"Laurel O'Hara."

"Laurel?" I looked at her. "We were going to name the baby Willow if it was a girl."

She shook her head stubbornly. "Cloudy Willow named her Laurel."

She slipped out, closing the door behind her. I was left alone with death, and with life.

As I sat there a great determination filled me. I had failed Cloudy Willow because her people hadn't grasped what I taught. But I wouldn't fail my baby daughter. I would go so far away from Vista d'Oro — which in a few moments I had learned to hate passionately — no one would ever find us. Never would I tell any living soul what had happened that day. I despised the ignorance, the superstition, the old customs that had taken my wife so needlessly. I would raise Laurel as white, with no knowledge of her Indian blood.

This is what I did. I brought you to

Phoenix when you were a week old. Not even our housekeeper, Mrs. Scott, knows your background. Never in any way have I let any person know the events of your birth.

Laurel, in time the hatred was replaced with compassion and understanding. Still, it hurt too much to speak of your mother. I was glad your eyes were blue like mine, yet you looked like her. I knew you wanted to know about her, but in time I think I filled your life until you really didn't have the crying need you might have felt.

Now I've broken my vow of silence. It is because of a letter I received. Remember the field day the newspapers had with my collapse? Evidently word gets around, and for the first time since I left Vista d'Oro with you, a contact was made — a letter. I trembled at the postmark and hid it until after I was alone. Why should I hear from anyone there after all these years? Yet a strange feeling gripped me even as I opened the envelope.

It was from a Dr. Cliff Barclay. Evidently the clinic stood empty for many years after I fled, then a few years ago Dr. Barclay stumbled across it in his search for a quiet spot of desert where he could have both privacy and challenge. Slowly the people began to respond.

Laurel, it was like hearing my own story over again! Dr. Barclay made friends with many of the Navajos, especially an old woman called Many Tears. She was sickly, and seemed troubled, but took a special interest in the doctor.

Last week when Dr. Barclay saw the picture of me in the paper, he showed it to her and asked if she remembered my being there. She clutched the paper and asked to keep it.

Later that night she sent for the doctor.

"I am old and ready to die. But before I meet the Great Spirit I must confess my sin."

"Would you like me to get the missionary?" Dr. Barclay asked. A new missionary has started a tiny church since the doctor came.

"No, no!" she cried wildly. "You must make things right!"

Not understanding, but unwilling to see the poor woman suffer, he told her, "Of course."

"Will you promise to tell no one until I am gone?" she asked.

"I promise."

Many Tears went on to tell the doctor a

strange story, the story of your birth, Laurel. Only the story didn't end there, as we thought. When she attended Cloudy Willow *not one, but two babies were born!* Cloudy Willow lived long enough to name one Laurel, the other Willow.

Many Tears knew I was to be back soon. She feared my anger and somehow knew I would never stay at Vista d'Oro without Cloudy Willow. What could she do? She had lost her only child.

A desperate plan began to form in her mind. No one knew there were two babies but her. She would steal one and leave the other. No one would ever know. There was another young woman whom she was to attend later that week. If all went well she would slip Willow into her room, and Willow would grow up in Vista d'Oro where Many Tears could see her every day.

Laurel, sometimes the chance taken in desperation pays off. It happened even as Many Tears planned. The only thing she hadn't counted on was that the other mother also would die. But in a way, this was even better.

"I will take this little one," she told the dazed father. "Her mother is gone, you do not know how to care for babies. I will

24

take her and name her Willow after my own daughter." Heartsick at losing his wife, the young man agreed, and so Willow became Many Tears's own.

All these years Many Tears had kept these things inside. Even when her husband, the chief, died she did not tell anyone. But now that it was her turn to ride the night wind she felt she had done wrong.

Dr. Barclay finished his letter by saying he didn't know how much, if any, Willow knew of the story. The village is very close-mouthed. Perhaps she knows none of it. But the fact remains, Laurel, you have a twin sister right now, living in Vista d'Oro!

I know this will be a shock to you, yet I am leaving you and, like Many Tears, I can't go without telling you the truth. If it hadn't been for my attack and Many Tears's conscience my vow would remain intact. As it is, I felt you had to know.

Since I've learned these things, my viewpoint is different. I realize that even if it weren't for Willow, you still had a right to know and be proud of your heritage. I was wrong to deprive you of such a background. Cloudy Willow and her people, yes, your people too, Laurel, are a race of valor and courage. There are those who won't see it like that, who may become cool if or when they discover your parentage, yet those Navajo people with their different way of life would stand head and shoulders above many in our Phoenix crowd.

Knowing you, I doubt that you'll be able to just ignore these things and go on in your same old way. But whatever you do, don't do it in haste! If you decide to look for Willow, you must accept that she either won't know you or will probably resent you disrupting her way of life. She may despise me or even hate you. In a way, it might be best just to leave things as they are now.

Yet, somehow I hope that someday you will find her. She's your twin, part of you. And if you do . . . tell her I didn't know . . . and ask her to forgive.

All my love,
Dad

Chapter 2

A shower of sparks from the breaking logs in the fireplace startled Laurel back into reality. There had been no need to reread her father's letter. She felt it was indelibly branded into her very soul. A twin sister, a Navajo twin sister! Laurel was torn by emotions new to her. Regret for the mother she had never known, incredulity that her father had never told her, curiosity about her twin, fear of the future. What should she do?

Leaving the couch, she paced the floor. There had been a plea in her father's letter, she sensed that. Did he want her to find Willow? Or was he warning her it would be best to forget? Yet how could she do that? She was no longer the Laurel O'Hara she had always thought she was. She was bone and blood of a proud Indian princess as well as sturdy O'Hara stock.

Suppose she tore up the letter and told no one? The only one who would ever know would be Dr. Barclay, and after all, who was he? Surely he would have little interest in her. A substantial gift to his precious Vista d'Oro clinic would probably buy his silence and her life could go on its uninterrupted way. No, no one would ever know — but herself. She paused before a long mirror, examining every feature, somehow expecting to find a change in her face, but the same smooth oval greeted her that always had.

At last in sheer exhaustion she went to bed, throwing herself down fully clothed. She was even too tired to undress. In a few moments she would shower and prepare for night. Now she would just rest a bit. But the strain had been too much, and soon she drifted into a troubled sleep. When she awoke a shaft of sunlight was stealing between the drawn drapes and she could hear the rattle of Mrs. Scott's key in the front door. Luckily the housekeeper had gone to her niece's for the weekend, Laurel thought. Even Mrs. Scott, dear as she was, mustn't be told until Laurel had decided what she was going to do.

Hastily brushing her hair and tying it back with a scarlet ribbon, Laurel showered and changed into a pants outfit and then went into the kitchen.

It was a lovely spot for a homemaker to work. The white walls stenciled with green leaves were reflected by the matching curtains. Green and white tile and bright copper pans gave a warmth to the room, and the nook with its small table and two chairs invited kitchen visitors. There was even a rocking chair where Laurel had spent many happy hours with Mrs. Scott.

"Land sakes, are you all right?" she demanded, looking anxiously into Laurel's pale face. "You look like you haven't slept for a week!"

"I've been tired ever since I went on night shift," Laurel answered truthfully, not explaining she hadn't worked the night before.

"You'd better get out in the fresh air today before you have to rest for tonight," Mrs. Scott told her. Then she added in a gentler voice, "Are you still fretting about your daddy?"

Laurel shook her head. "No, he wouldn't want that. That's why I stick to the bright colors he loved. He hated black."

"Good," Mrs. Scott said with satisfaction. "Now sit down and eat something, that'll perk you up."

Laurel was sure she couldn't swallow a mouthful but didn't want to hurt Mrs. Scott, so she dutifully pecked at her scrambled eggs and toast, even managing to finish her orange juice. Jane Scott was a dear. Small and bird-like, she had come when Laurel was a baby. Never had a real mother lavished more love and attention on anyone than she did on Laurel. Yet she had old-fashioned ideas about discipline and re-spect and had seen to it that Laurel wasn't spoiled by all the attention she had received by being her father's daughter.

In spite of her own misery, Laurel watched Mrs. Scott curiously and then asked, "How did you happen to come to us?"

Mrs. Scott turned in surprise. "Why, you needed me, dearie, and I needed a job. I re-member when your father advertised for someone. He sat behind that big desk and I was so afraid I wouldn't get the job. I needed it desperately. My husband and little girl had been killed in an accident a few months before and there was no money coming in."

Laurel gasped. She had never even thought to ask about Mrs. Scott's family. She had always just taken for granted that Mrs. Scott belonged to the O'Haras.

Mrs. Scott went on. "A lot of others ap-plied, but when I told him about Ben and Mary, your daddy looked right into my eyes. 'Mrs. Scott, I think we need each other.' That's all there was to it. I came, and I stayed." She wiped a tear away on the hem of her apron.

"After all these years, Laurel, what made you ask?"

Laurel avoided replying directly.

"Oh, I don't know," she answered vaguely, then added, "I think I'll take that walk now." She could feel Mrs. Scott's gaze on her as she slipped out the patio doors and walked toward the nearby park.

It was good to be out. Phoenix was never more beautiful to her than in early fall. Already a few leaves were beginning to show color, and there was a haze in the distance. It wasn't so hot as it had been, either.

I wonder what autumn is like in Vista d'Oro? she thought idly, then sharply brought her attention back to the stoplight warning her not to cross. Reaching the park entrance, she slowly walked the paths, not seeing much, yet sensing the quietness that somehow seemed to still her racing mind.

I'd like to go away. The realization startled her, yet the intensity of it brought bright flashes of color to her cheeks. One part of her scoffed. You can't get away. You've only been at Mountainside a year, and they were so nice about letting you take time when your dad was sick. How can you ask for a vacation now? But from deep inside another voice seemed to insist, You need peace and rest. Even these short moments alone with nature have helped restore your balance.

Pushing the thoughts into the background, Laurel walked to a nearby bench and dropped down. There was a small artificial pond near and ducks swimming round and round in an everlasting circle, getting nowhere.

That's me, she thought. I'm in a little circle going round and round. I never realized it before but I've never really been anywhere but Phoenix. I haven't even seen my own state. All the years of growing up Dad was too busy, and since then my nurse's training and job have kept me occupied.

Suddenly she felt tired, drained, depressed.

She went back to the house and told Mrs. Scott she was going to take a nap. Yet after lowering the blinds she lay wide-eyed, staring at the ceiling, going over again in her mind the whole story and thinking, If I could only put my finger on the one thing that's bothering me most.

Is it because I've discovered I'm half Navajo? That doesn't change the fact I'm me. Is it because I resent having to share Dad with a sister? But that can't be it, for he's gone. Is it because I don't know how people will react? She squirmed uncomfortably, knowing she was getting closer to the truth. Finally she admitted it to herself. Her chief concern was what Dr. Grant Carson would think if he knew. But you don't have to tell him, a little voice whispered.

Shame filled her. If her father had been so proud of her mother, how could she feel Grant would reject her because of that heritage? If he loved her, it wouldn't make any difference. But did he?

Tossing and turning, Laurel finally slipped into the bathroom and took one of the mild sedatives they had given her after her father's death. It had been weeks now since she had had one, but she must sleep. She had to work tonight and then tomorrow was her day off. She had to rest.

Several hours later Mrs. Scott knocked gently at the door and at Laurel's groggy "Come in" apologetically explained, "I hate to disturb you, Laurel, but young Dr. Carson is on the phone. He says he must speak to you."

"It's all right, Mrs. Scott." Laurel pushed her hair back. "I need to get up anyway. Why, it's five o'clock! I've slept all afternoon."

"Yes, and you needed it." Mrs. Scott plugged in the extension phone before leaving the room.

Laurel caught sight of her reflection in the mirrored dressing table as she picked up the phone. No lack of color now — she was positively glowing.

"Hello, Grant."

"Hello, darling," the cool, assured voice came over the wire. "Mrs. Murray said you didn't report in last night and I've wondered about you all day. You aren't sick, are you?"

Quick tears filled her eyes at his concern as the whole miserable business swept over her again.

"No," she managed to say. "I'm all right now."

He was silent for a moment, then asked, "Would you be able to see me for a little while tonight before going on duty? Wear your uniform and we'll eat in a quiet place. I can take you to the hospital later." He paused for a moment, then went on. "There's something I have to ask you right away. I had planned to wait, but . . ." His voice trailed off.

Laurel's heart jumped to her throat. Was it possible he knew about her? Don't be ridiculous, she told herself angrily. There's no way he could. Nevertheless her heart was in her voice as she told him, "I can be ready in three quarters of an hour."

"Good. I'll pick you up then." There was a sharp click and the connection was broken.

"Mrs. Scott," Laurel called. "I'm going out for dinner."

Mrs. Scott appeared in the doorway. "I thought as much." Her voice was sharp. "Can't he ever call earlier, instead of waiting until the last minute? I have a roast nearly ready. Would he want to eat here?"

"I don't think so. He said he had something to ask me."

"So that's it." Mrs. Scott seated herself on the edge of the bed as Laurel donned her uniform.

"Laurel." There was something in Mrs. Scott's voice that caught Laurel's attention immediately. Mrs. Scott looked at the tall, beautiful girl in white, affection filling her eyes, then determinedly said, "Laurel, young Dr. Carson will ask you to marry him, if not tonight, then one of these days. Are you in love with him?"

Laurel looked at her soberly, sensing the deep concern behind the question. A half blush touched her smooth face as she replied seriously, "I don't know. He's handsome, considerate, and we have a lot in common. In addition, I feel attracted to him. Does that mean I'm in love? Sometimes I think so, but then marriage seems such a big step that other times I don't know whether I want Grant 'for keeps' or not."

Her voice trembled.

"Mrs. Scott, is there something wrong with me? Isn't all that enough?"

"No!" The sharpness of the quick reply rang in the room. "No, Laurel, being attracted to a handsome, courteous man is not enough! You are just old-fashioned enough in your ways to want a man just as you said, 'for keeps.' If you do, then there's a lot more to marriage than what you've just named. The best there is isn't too much to expect, and until you know you can't be happy anywhere except where that certain one is, don't promise to marry. When the time comes you'd not only promise to go to the ends of the earth with that special someone, but you'd promise *gladly — and with no reservations*. Then you know it's the right kind of love."

Laurel was taken aback by the vehemence of Mrs. Scott's answer, then she asked shyly, "Was that the kind of love you had?"

The housekeeper's features softened in remembrance. "Yes, Laurel. Even though my marriage was short, it was as near perfect as two people could make it. We didn't have much money, but I wouldn't trade those few years together for anything else I know. When I lost Ben and Mary I didn't know if I could keep on living. I wondered

36

why I hadn't been taken too, along with them. Then your daddy hired me and I realized my work here wasn't done. I had another reason to live — you. That's why I couldn't keep still today. I want you to have the kind of marriage I had, and the kind your parents had."

"My parents! Did Dad talk to you about his marriage?" Laurel was astounded.

Mrs. Scott shook her head. "He didn't need to, Laurel. When a man as handsome as Mike O'Hara evades all the pursuing females for all those years and doesn't even have any interest in them, it shows his marriage must have been pretty special. He doesn't need to talk about it."

Through Laurel's mind flashed the words from the letter: ". . . a perfect mating . . . blending of lives and personalities until we were like two blades creating one pair of scissors." Mrs. Scott was right. That's the kind of marriage Laurel wanted, too.

"I won't say yes until I'm sure," she promised.

Mrs. Scott gave her a quick hug, then pulled back to cover her emotion. "Land sakes, I'm messing up your clean uniform. There's young Dr. Carson now," she added as the doorbell chimed.

Perhaps it was Mrs. Scott's words that

caused Laurel at the last moment to slip her father's letter into her handbag. It gave her a strange sense of security, mixed with trepidation. During the excellent dinner Laurel had opportunity to study her companion. His dark eyes and hair complemented her own rich coloring, and they made a handsome couple despite her simple uniform. Grant was aware of and amused by the glances of several other patrons when they entered the restaurant.

"Certainly pays to have a pretty girl with you," he murmured as the headwaiter led them to a secluded table overlooking the lights of Phoenix. Laurel disciplined a grin and smiled charmingly at the waiter instead.

When dinner was over Grant leaned forward and asked seriously, "Laurel, you're fond of me, aren't you?"

Shocked at the intensity of his tone, Laurel replied, "Of course, Grant. You know that."

A smile of satisfaction lit up his countenance and he leaned back in his chair.

"I'm glad to hear that. I have some fantastic news for you. I've been offered a chance at your father's hospital when my residency is over. It will lead to Chief Surgeon position in time."

A flood of feeling swept over Laurel.

Grant in her father's job! A moment later she was ashamed and managed to cover her hesitation by exclaiming, "Why, Grant, that's wonderful! When did you hear?"

"Just this morning. That's why I was so anxious to see you tonight." He reached in his pocket and took out a small heart-shaped box. As he touched the spring, a beautiful blue-white solitaire diamond ring shimmered in the candlelight.

"The good news gave me the courage to put a down-payment on this today."

Laurel gasped in amazement. A stone like that must have cost a fortune! Luckily Grant was too immersed in his own plans to notice her reaction.

"What do you say, Laurel? Will you wear it?" A look of anxiety crossed his face. "You said you were fond of me and just think, in a few years we'll be top of the ladder here in Phoenix. You know how Chief Surgeon is looked up to and a good R.N. is always appreciated. It sure doesn't hurt any that you're Doc O'Hara's kid, either!"

For a moment a strange thought touched Laurel. He hadn't said one word about loving her. Some of this must have shown in her eyes, for he suddenly beckoned the waiter.

"Let's get out of here. This is no place for

a proposal." A few moments later they were in the car parked among the date palms behind the restaurant. No one else was around and Grant, almost fiercely, took Laurel in his arms, his mouth crushing down on hers. A thrill shot through her. Grant really cared this much? Her promise to Mrs. Scott was forgotten in the wild beating of her heart.

"Oh, Grant, do you really love me?"

"Sure, Laurel. Everybody knows I'm crazy about you." He sat back with a look of triumph in his eyes. "That's my girl, I knew you'd say yes."

A strange lack in his words came through to Laurel for a moment, but she put it firmly aside. He had said he was crazy about her, hadn't he? It was probably hard for the words 'I love you' to come natural to Grant, modern sophisticate that he was. She leaned against him. How happy her father would be to know she had found such a perfect mate. Her father! In consternation she sat up straight.

"Wait, Grant, I have to tell you something before you put the ring on." He stopped short, a sharp line cutting between his brows.

"My father . . ." She couldn't go on. Then she remembered the letter. It would be the best. She forced it into his hands, causing him to drop the beautiful ring in her lap

"Before I can wear this" — she picked up the ring and handed it to him — "you must read this letter. Then if you still want to marry me, I will."

"What do I care about some old letter?" he demanded. "What could it possibly have to do with us?"

"It has everything to do with us," she responded gravely. "If you will read it tonight we can talk about it tomorrow."

Seeing the seriousness of her face he didn't persist, but folded the letter angrily and put it in his pocket.

"All right, have it your way. I'll read it tonight. But tomorrow morning at seven, I'll be there to pick you up from work. I have the day off, and we can start making plans for our wedding and honeymoon."

Seeing how downcast she had grown, the anger left his voice. "Cheer up, Laurel, I won't beat you, no matter what's in the letter."

She smiled wanly and told him, "If I don't get to the hospital, Mrs. Murray will."

Both of them were silent, under a strain, as he threaded his way through the late traffic and pulled up at the nurse's entrance to Mountainside. With a quick glance to see no one was watching, Grant kissed her good night.

"See you tomorrow," he promised. With a wave of a hand, he was gone, leaving her alone on the steps, filled with a strange foreboding of what tomorrow would bring.

Chapter 3

Never had an eight-hour duty shift gone so slowly. Laurel was not one to let personal problems interfere with her work, yet she found herself counting the minutes. She quietly and efficiently performed her duties, responding to Mrs. Murray and her best friend, Beth, with a simple, "Yes, I'm all right." Seeing her pallor they were unconvinced, yet neither would intrude on her privacy. When Laurel was ready to talk, she would come to one of them.

As Laurel slipped in and out of the children's rooms, small pocket flash in hand, she realized what a blessing work was. When one is involved in routine duties there is no time for personal problems, she thought, and was comforted. She was pleased to see two of her favorite small patients had gone home that day and another was scheduled for dismissal tomorrow. Laurel loved children and hoped to have several. She wondered if Grant liked children, but sternly forced thought of him aside. There was no time for personal thoughts on night shift. Her time and attention were for the children only. She had no right to think of other things.

Finally the shift ended. True to his word, Grant was waiting when she got off duty. Grim and thin-lipped, he little resembled the handsome suitor of the previous night. He silently helped her into the shining yellow sports car and headed for a favorite early-morning spot just outside town where they could be alone.

Laurel didn't know what to say. Her heart beat painfully, and she stole a sidewise look at him. He showed traces of a sleepless night, and her heart sank. Beyond question she knew he had not been able to accept the truth about her. A rush of bitterness shot through her. She just hadn't realized how much she cared until now that it was too late.

When they were parked back from the road he switched off the ignition and turned to her.

"I read your father's rather remarkable letter." He paused, as though searching for words. "It does put a different light on things, doesn't it?"

Miserably Laurel nodded. "That's why I asked you to read it." Some of her emptiness communicated itself to him.

"Laurel, it won't make any difference to us. What's past is past. It has nothing to do with you and me."

Laurel felt as though she had emerged from sunless day to a field of brilliant sunshine. "It doesn't make any difference?" she asked wonderingly. "It really won't affect us at all?"

"Of course not," he assured her, gathering her into his arms.

This is heaven, she thought. This is where I belong, with a man so understanding and kind. She had been so tired, it was good just to lean against him. For a long time she was content not to even move, then his words pierced her consciousness and brought her upright on the seat, almost unable to grasp his meaning.

"What did you say, Grant?"

He reached for her again, laughing. "No one will ever know anything about it, Laurel. I brought the letter and you can take it home and burn it. Why should something from long ago even be remembered? We'll adopt our children instead of having them natural born —"

"I don't understand," she interrupted. "What are you talking about?"

He looked at her steadily. "Of course you do, Laurel. If we don't want people to know about your mother we can't have children. There's always the chance of a throwback.

We wouldn't want that."

"I see," Laurel managed to say through the waves of nausea rising within her at his cold calculations. "Then no one will ever know about my mother or Vista d'Oro or Willow? Just like before Dad wrote the letter?"

Grant's face brightened. "That's right, darling. You're so sensible. It's not that I mind myself, you know. It's that so many people are narrow-minded, and there would be the usual amount of gossip. It could really hurt my chances at Desert General. They'd just never understand how your father could . . ." His expressive shrug completed the sentence.

For a moment Laurel thought she was going to be sick. Understanding Grant! What a laugh! All the time he had this in mind. She could see he had evidently spent the rest of the night after reading the letter making plans.

He was so pleased with himself. He wanted her not for her love but because she was Doc O'Hara's kid, as he had put it, because it would help him get ahead. Get ahead and into her own father's job? The father he now spoke of so lightly.

"I think I'd like to go home now," she told him. Glancing at her pale, set face,

46

he agreed readily.

"I didn't bring your ring this morning. I knew you'd be too tired and upset to enjoy it. Why don't I pick you up this evening and we'll really celebrate. You have tomorrow off, don't you?"

Laurel replied steadily, "Yes, I have tomorrow off." Inside she added, But you won't be seeing me, tomorrow or ever. What a fool I was to think my heritage wouldn't make any difference! How I hate him! Smug, so sure I'd fall in with his plans. Adopt children so no one would ever know who I really am!

A fierce pride of her newly discovered race rose within Laurel. Raising her head proudly, she smiled above her broken dreams and murmured softly, "Yes, Grant, I'll be off tomorrow." He looked at her oddly, seeming to catch a hidden meaning, but said no more.

When they arrived home she ran from the car up the steps before he could open the door for her. "Good-bye, Grant."

She stood watching the yellow car and Grant drive away out of her life. Anger filled her, blunting the disappointment she had felt when her bubble burst. Perhaps later she could think of him rationally, not now. She must get away, and soon. The feeling of the day before in the park filled her again and quickened her steps as she burst into the kitchen. Mrs. Scott was just cutting a pan of warm chocolate brownies fresh from the oven. Their fragrance filled the air.

"Mrs. Scott," Laurel blurted out. "How would you like to go on a trip?"

"A trip? Oh, I don't know." She smiled, knife still poised above the brownies. "I'd rather just stay here with you, dearie."

"I mean with me," Laurel announced. "I don't care where, just so we get away from Phoenix for a while."

Mrs. Scott looked at Laurel in compassion. "Is it that bad?"

"Yes, no, oh, I don't know!" Laurel stammered, twisting a fold of her uniform skirt between nervous fingers.

Mrs. Scott put down the knife and folded her arms across her aproned front. "Do you want to tell me about it, Laurel?" She seated herself in the rocker.

Suddenly a great longing went through Laurel. What better person to listen to the whole story than Jane Scott, whose loving counsel down through the years had always been both fair and wise? With a quick rush, Laurel dropped to her knees in front of the rocker and buried her face in Mrs. Scott's lap. Muffled sobs that she had held back ever since her father had died now shook her slender body.

"There, there," Mrs. Scott crooned. "He isn't worth all that."

Quick as a flash Laurel's head was lifted. "You think I'm crying for Grant? Oh, no, Mrs. Scott, it's not him. I don't even know where to start!"

For a long moment the good woman was silent, gently stroking the midnight-black hair, then she slowly said, "I think perhaps, Laurel, you had better begin with your beautiful mother."

With an exclamation of mingled surprise and relief Laurel sat up.

"You know! Oh, Mrs. Scott, I'm so glad! But how did you find out?"

"Yes, Laurel," Mrs. Scott replied softly. "I've known since the first year I came to you. Dr. O'Hara had a week-long convention when you were just a year old. It gave me a chance to clean in every nook and cranny without bothering him. Like most men, he hated a house torn up even for necessary cleaning.

"As I moved boxes around in his closet the cord holding one broke, spilling the contents on the floor. I didn't mean to pry but when I picked up the documents and papers a photograph slipped from between two pieces of cardboard. It was of your father and a beautiful young girl in Navajo costume.

"I knew then why Dr. O'Hara had no interest in women except as friends. She was lovely, the image of you, except with soft brown eyes instead of the O'Hara blue. I felt Dr. O'Hara's reasons for keeping the picture hidden, whatever they were, were not for me to know. I could only guess that some tragedy had taken her from him. Because of my own loss I knew and respected his silent sorrow, so I carefully put everything back on the shelf and said nothing. All these years I've known, but if he had reason to keep things from you, I had no right to question."

She paused, then asked, "But how did you find out after all this time, Laurel?"

Very slowly Laurel took out the letter from her purse. "Mrs. Scott, I think I'd like you to read this."

Mrs. Scott's sharp eyes missed little. "Did young Dr. Carson see this?"

"Yes, he did," Laurel admitted, meeting Mrs. Scott's look directly.

"I thought so." Her tone was dry. Going to the breakfast nook for her glasses, she sat down at the table and spread the closely written pages before her.

Too nervous to sit still, Laurel drifted to the living room. Her favorite Strauss waltz album was on the stereo, and she switched it on. "The Blue Danube" filled the room. It had been playing the night she first met Grant Carson at the country club. It seemed a million years in the past. So complete had been her disillusionment that the only thing she now felt was contempt. Not only for him, but for herself. How could he believe her such a spineless creature that she would go along with all his plans? That she would agree to a monstrous deception?

Yet, forcing herself to face things honestly, that was what she too had thought of in the beginning. Now there seemed to be no question. She couldn't ignore that letter.

Somehow since Mrs. Scott's knowledge had come to light, it was easier for Laurel. Just knowing Mrs. Scott had partly shared the secret all those years seemed to help.

It took Mrs. Scott a long time to read the letter. When she finally came to the living room, an unaccustomed mist was in her eyes.

"Thank you for sharing this, Laurel. In spite of all the tragedy, it is still a beautiful letter and one you should treasure. Can you realize now the kind of marriage I want for you?" She paused for a moment. "Young

51

Dr. Carson didn't see it that way, did he?"

Laurel met her question head on. "No, he didn't. He suggested I burn the letter and we would adopt our children so no one could ever say anything that would reflect on him while he gets Dad's Chief Surgeon job at Desert General."

At her bald statement of facts Mrs. Scott became too furious to hold her tongue. "Why, the spalpeen! Reflect on him, would it? Nothing could reflect so badly on him as his own conceit and snobbery!"

Laurel couldn't help but laugh at her indignation.

"You never did like him, did you Mrs. Scott?"

"No, I didn't! Too big for his britches, I'd say!" She clapped her hand over her mouth too late to stifle the words, but her brown eyes sparkled defiantly. "You shouldn't have asked me that!"

"Yes, I should," Laurel responded. "And I must say I agree with you." The laugh that followed relieved tension for them both. Then Mrs. Scott sobered.

"Now what, Laurel?"

Laurel was completely motionless for a long time, then she spoke with a faraway look in her eyes. "I think I'm going to find my sister."

Mrs. Scott nodded. "I thought you would. I think your father would be pleased." She riffled the pages in her hand. "But remember what he said?" She read aloud, "But whatever you do, don't do it in haste!"

She went on, "I like your idea of a trip. You've seen so little. Why don't we go? Autumn in Arizona is beautiful." A longing look crept into her eyes.

"The Grand Canyon. White Mountains. Oak Creek Canyon. Oh, Laurel, you'll love them all. There will be peace and quiet, time to think. Time to consider what's the best thing to do about Willow." Her eyes glistened, then her practical side took over again.

"When do you want to go?"

Laurel smiled, catching something of her eagerness. "Today."

"Today!" Mrs. Scott threw her hands up in the air, then slowly smiled. "Young Dr. Carson was coming tonight, wasn't he?" and at Laurel's nod of assent, she added, "Yes, I think you're right. We'll leave today." She glanced at the clock.

"Mercy! Ten o'clock! We'll have to work fast. You go pack enough clothes, including a lot of warm things, so we won't have to come back until we want to. I'll call and get the electricity and telephone disconnected

53

and a lunch put up. We won't have time to eat now. You had your car serviced just last week, didn't you?"

"Yes," Laurel replied. "It was completely gone over."

Mrs. Scott briskly started to the kitchen, then stopped dead still. "What about Mountainside?"

Laurel replied evenly. "I'll call them first. Mrs. Murray will waive the notice if she can and give me an indefinite leave of absence. I know she's worried about me. If she can't, then I'll quit."

A look of complete agreement crossed Mrs. Scott's face. "Burn all your bridges. That's best." She started for the kitchen again only to stick her head back in. "Don't forget those warm clothes. It can be cold in the mountains."

By four o'clock Laurel couldn't believe what had been accomplished. The house was ready to be closed, an extra key left with the nearest neighbor in case of emergency. The post office was holding their mail until further notice. Mrs. Murray had been as un-derstanding as Laurel hoped, telling her to take all the time she needed. Laurel's suit-case and purse were loaded with travelers' checks. Thank heavens Dad had left her well provided for! She had enough to carry her through a long time without having to work, and Mrs. Scott confessed she would rob her savings account if Laurel needed it. This brought the tears again, and Laurel assured her there was enough for both, there was no need for Mrs. Scott's savings.

At last they were ready. The white Mustang was packed to the brim with suitcases and all the leftover food in the house in case they didn't want to stop for a while. It was a beautiful evening for driving. They could put a lot of miles behind them before night if they chose.

Laurel was taking one last look around the living room, wondering when they would see it again, thrilled at her expedition, when Mrs. Scott came in with a thin tissue-wrapped package. Together they folded back the tissue paper and for the first time Laurel gazed into her mother's eyes.

Cloudy Willow! How lovely! And what a handsome couple she and Mike O'Hara had been.

Tears blurred Laurel's vision as she carefully re-wrapped the picture and placed it in her overnight case. Turning, she took Mrs. Scott's hands in her own.

"How can I ever thank you . . . for everything?" She couldn't go on.

Mrs. Scott smiled tenderly. "Why don't

you start by calling me Aunt Jane?" Wordlessly Laurel nodded. She locked the front door, and they silently climbed in the Mustang. Their future lay ahead, not behind, and as they drove away, neither looked back.

Promptly at six o'clock Dr. Grant Carson's yellow sports car stopped in front of the O'Hara residence. Strange, all the blinds were pulled tightly. Striding to the front door, he rang the bell, but no one answered. The whole place appeared to be deserted. He noticed the shutters were pulled from the inside and evidently latched shut. Where could Laurel be? Surely she couldn't have disappeared in the short time since he had left her there that morning.

Mr. Neilson from next door called over the gate, "She's gone away, doctor."

Not for the world would the young doctor have the neighbors know he had been unaware of Laurel's plans. Swallowing an angry retort he flashed his brilliant smile.

"Oh, she did get off! I was hoping I could get here before she left."

Mr. Neilson's cackle told Dr. Carson his little ruse hadn't worked. "You can write her in care of General Delivery, Doc." His odious laughter made the doctor even more furious as he slammed into his car and shot out into the street, narrowly missing a little boy on a tricycle.

There was going to be the dickens to pay, he knew that. One of the reasons he had been selected for the place at Desert General was his supposed intimacy with Laurel. That's why he had been so anxious to get the ring on her finger before the final Board meeting. Now she was gone without a trace.

Stopping at the nearest phone booth, he tried several times to call but got nothing. In desperation he dialed the operator, who told him, "I'm sorry, sir, that number has been disconnected." Defeated, he again slammed into his car. Had she been offended that morning? He thought he had handled things pretty well. Tactful, yet making himself clear. She had always seemed so tractable. After all, it was a bit shattering to find out the girl you had selected for your wife because of her social position and wealth of friends suddenly turned up with, shall we say, undesirable relatives. What more could he have done?

Remembering her beauty and response, he cursed himself for a fool. Maybe he should have been a little more gentle with her, but if he had, who knows but what next she would want to be out hunting up that twin sister.

His eyes narrowed. The twin sister! That's it, he exulted. What was the name of that dinky Indian village where the clinic had been? He couldn't remember. No matter, he had a good road map at home. It wouldn't take long for him to find out. He would go after her and get things straightened out immediately. Maybe he could even overtake her.

No, on second thought, if he started running after her now, it would always be that way. He would send a letter to be given to her as soon as she reached the village.

He smiled unpleasantly. In the long run it would be best for her to know who was the boss in their relationship. Yes, he would send her a message that would bring her back posthaste if that's where she had gone.

A cold feeling seemed to steal over him for a moment. His plans were fine, if that's where she had gone. But if she hadn't? What then? His future depended in large part upon finding her, and finding her soon. Tomorrow he would begin making casual inquiries among her friends and at the hospital. He had to find Laurel, and quick! Once he did, he could make her pay for all the trouble she was causing him by running off when she knew how important it was to him for her to be there.

Chapter 4

While Dr. Carson was frantically trying to track down Laurel and growing more upset by the moment, the object of his search was leisurely driving east on Highway 60.

It was a new experience for both Laurel and Jane Scott. There was no need for words between them; both were exhilarated by the taste of freedom. The sun was at their backs and after leaving Phoenix the traffic had thinned out, so Laurel could look around a bit as well as drive.

Mrs. Scott, now "Aunt Jane," was busily marking a road map. Laurel had told her to plan their "wanderings," as she called them. She was trying to remember all the beautiful places from the past that might appeal to the girl beside her.

A few moments before reaching Superior Laurel swung the Mustang off the right side of the road where a sign for the Southwestern Arboretum had caught her eye.

"Mrs. . . . Aunt Jane," she corrected herself. "Let's stop and see everything there is along the way."

Aunt Jane agreed. "I hope it's still open."

The caretaker reluctantly let them in,

glancing at his watch pointedly. "Almost closing time," he grumbled, but Laurel and Aunt Jane did have time for a quick tour.

When they were back in the car Laurel bubbled over, "That's the first time I've ever been out here! There's so much I haven't done. Oh, Aunt Jane, this is going to be a wonderful vacation!" The look of strain she had worn so long seemed lifted, but her companion knew how tired Laurel could become so when they reached Globe she suggested stopping for the night.

They found a motel on a quiet side street. Laurel shook her head at the more popular ones.

"I'd rather stay in a simple, clean cabin away from so many people."

Aunt Jane realized she was afraid of running into someone who might recognize and question her. Carefully they unpacked the well-prepared hampers and ice chest. Their supper of fried chicken, potato salad, pickles, and the brownies was delicious. Laurel was surprised by her appetite. The cool air certainly had done something for her.

The big window of their cabin faced west and as they ate, they watched the sun set. Laurel never failed to marvel how one moment it was there and the next it was gone. That was one of the things she loved about the wide open country. You could almost hear a "kerplunk" when it dropped out of sight. They sat quietly until the last crimson, rose, and saffron streak of after-glow left the sky, and then with a yawn Laurel said, "I think we'd better go to bed!"

Within moments after showering and crawling between the sheets, Laurel was asleep. The fresh air, quiet, and good food had done their work well. There was no lying awake for her that night.

Aunt Jane looked at the beautiful girl asleep, then gently closed the door and went to her own room. Before sleeping she knelt by her bedside and asked that Laurel be given strength for whatever lay ahead. Then she too slept.

Laurel awakened very early the next morning. Her screened window was open and a bird was singing his heart out. Sun-shine flooded the room as she quietly slipped from bed and opened the curtains. Strange, she mused. It all seemed unreal. Her father's letter, Grant's reaction — none of it seemed so terribly important now. She recognized it would all be there to be faced, but for now it was enough to appreciate the day and her new-found freedom.

This is a moment I will cherish, she

thought. In the distance were chimes of a carillon, telling the world it was a Sabbath morning. How long since Sunday had meant anything to her! Because of the odd shifts she and her father worked, it had become just another day in their lives.

In quick determination she pattered to Aunt Jane's door in her bare feet, the cloud of dark hair about her shoulders. Aunt Jane was already dressed, enjoying the view from her window as Laurel had done.

"I'd like to go to church," she said shyly.

Aunt Jane's face lit up. "What a wonderful idea! Yes, let's go."

Dressed in white following a simple breakfast, Laurel brushed her shining hair into a pageboy and they were ready. Jane was crisp and cool in a green print. Laurel had noticed a small, white "friendly looking" church on the edge of town and wanted to go there.

It was a simple service, such as are held in hundreds of churches every Sunday morning. The hymns were sung enthusiastically, ones Laurel remembered from childhood. She and Aunt Jane both blinked back tears, recalling days when Dr. O'Hara hadn't been so busy and the three of them sometimes attended church together.

Laurel had almost forgotten the strength

gained from worship. She listened intently to the scripture, "I will lift up mine eyes unto the hills from whence cometh my help." She wondered why so many of her friends scoffed at the idea of church. Morning light streamed through the stained-glass window behind the pulpit filling the chapel with muted colors. The sermon was short and to the point. The white-haired minister spoke of the peace and strength available for daily living for those who would accept it. Laurel felt he was speaking directly to her and took comfort. The lines in the minister's face showed he had known sorrow, yet they only gave credence to the truths he presented.

Laurel glanced at her companion. Aunt Jane had also known sorrow, but there was a calmness of spirit surrounding her. Would she ever be like Aunt Jane? She hoped so. After all, her father had believed in her and with Aunt Jane beside her nothing could be too hard to face.

The warmth of the congregation's greetings after the service touched Laurel. They were so sincerely happy she and Aunt Jane could be with them.

"We're just passing through," she told the minister wistfully. "But if we ever are back again, we'll come." The minister's kindly gaze followed the young girl and her companion as they went to the white Mustang. Sighing, he turned to the next of his congregation, remembering the look of trouble in her eyes that was replaced by hope during his sermon. He must pray for that girl. Then he remembered she hadn't even told him her name.

The sun was high overhead as Laurel and Aunt Jane left Globe. They had decided to swing southeast to Safford, then north into the White Mountains. The scenery wasn't very interesting for the first several miles but neither noticed. The morning service had brought a closeness that had been missing since Laurel grew up. Now she felt like the little girl who used to tag behind Mrs. Scott from room to room, asking questions, just to be with her. The last few years had been too busy for such close contact. It wasn't until now Laurel realized how much she had missed it.

It was enough for Aunt Jane just to be with her beloved charge. There were a hundred things to talk about. She told Laurel little bits of her own life while Laurel was constantly saying, "Do you remember . . ." and off they would go again. It was a catching-up time. Before they knew it the desert lay behind, and they had turned off onto

Highway 666 that led through the Apache National Forest into the White Mountains. It was cooler now. Scrubby cedars gave way to larger trees. A riot of color appeared. Red-barked Ponderosa pine with their green needles provided an effective background for silvery birches and quivering aspen. Leaves were beginning to fall, and a golden carpet covered the forest floor.

Laurel had never seen such a place. The same intense blue sky she loved in Phoenix still smiled at her, but such a different world!

Mile after mile they traveled, then an unexpected detour switched them onto a country road for a few miles. It passed a new motel, only about a dozen cabins in all, with a tiny stream nearby. Most of the cabins didn't seem occupied and Aunt Jane smiled as Laurel slowed, then stopped. It was perfect. The cabins were peeled yellow pine, sweet smelling.

A young woman about Laurel's age showed them the cabin nearest the stream. Although small, it was adequately equipped and spotlessly clean. A tiny fireplace was decorated with fall leaves, and a bright Indian rug lay on the polished board floor in front of it.

"We'll take it," Laurel said impulsively,

not even asking the price. The motelkeeper, whose name was Carol Parker, smiled at her enthusiasm and told her, "There's a small restaurant in the back of our store when you get hungry."

Laurel couldn't believe it, but suddenly she was ravenous again. The food was home-cooked, served on cheap dishes, but from the fresh vegetable salad from the garden to the sizzling steak and hot apple pie, everything was delicious.

That evening Laurel and Aunt Jane sat on the porch of Carol's home, a sturdy peeled log house about twice the size of the motel cabins. Her husband, Tom, was locking the store for the night. He was a quiet, pleasant man a few years older than Carol. They had quite an unusual story. Shortly after they were married Tom's father had a heart attack. He pulled through fine but needed more rest than he could get at Pinyon Village, as he called the new motel he and his wife had started. Tom and Carol talked him into taking over their real-estate business in Tucson while they came to Pinyon Village. If he felt like coming back in the spring, they would go home, but secretly hoped they could stay.

"I'd like to spend the rest of my life here," Carol confided. "We usually have more activity, but right now the detour has been a nuisance. It goes off tomorrow and some of our 'regulars' will be drifting in."

Laurel looked at her curiously. "Won't you be lonesome this winter? I saw several high mountains. Surely you get snow."

Carol laughed happily. "Winter is a favorite time for many of Pinyon Village's regulars. Besides —" she glanced at her husband coming up the walk and added softly, "I could never be lonely when I have Tom."

Laurel was silenced. She contrasted Carol's face with the driving ambition of her friends in Phoenix. A pang of envy shot through her. What would it be like to be Carol? To live here in a spot literally carved from the forest, yet completely content to stay forever with the man you loved? She tried to picture Grant here and failed utterly. He would be bored in a day.

The thought depressed her. She had been so excited making her getaway from all she knew that the split with Grant had lain dormant. Although her idol had fallen, still she couldn't help think of what might have been, if Grant had only been different.

She rose abruptly. "I think I'll go to bed." Bidding the others good night, she turned and waved from the cabin's doorway.

A short time later Aunt Jane brought her a glass of warm milk, "To make you sleep, honey. Good night."

"Good night, Aunt Jane."

The kindness soothed Laurel more than the milk. The last thing she remembered was the wind in the pines outside her cabin.

When she awoke her depression was gone. A noise outside the window made her pull the curtain back in time to see two small striped chipmunks playing tag on the windowsill. When they saw her they scolded and disappeared into the big pine next to the cabin, only to reappear on the flat stones that made a natural bridge across the stream. A faint trail led up the opposite bank. Laurel's eyes widened as a deer daintily stepped down to drink, seemingly unafraid of the delighted girl at the window.

"Ohh," she breathed in wonder as Aunt Jane came in. "Can we stay longer?"

Aunt Jane looked at the map she had marked, a slight frown between her brows. "Yes, just so we're at the Grand Canyon when I managed to get the reservation. They barely managed to squeeze us in at all."

For three days they stayed with the Parkers, Aunt Jane contentedly knitting on the wide front porch, Laurel exploring every path around. Then reluctantly they bid the Parkers good-bye, promising to return someday. Aunt Jane had offered to drive, and Laurel was free to look out the window.

Presently she turned. "Carol has the most beautiful house I've ever seen." Aunt Jane glanced at her in surprise.

Seeing the quick look Laurel hastily explained, "I love ours, but somehow the Parkers' is more of a home. Maybe it's because they do everything together." Her tone was wistful. "Carol said they really had to save for the little stereo. She made the frilly curtains and they did all the painting themselves." She stopped, then finished with, "It's because their home has been furnished with love."

A faint mist touched Aunt Jane's eyes, but she only said, "I'm glad you understand that, Laurel."

Several minutes later Laurel took up the conversation as if there had been no pause. "I could never have had that with Grant, could I, Aunt Jane?"

The good woman shook her head. "I'm afraid not."

"I think I always realized it way down deep; I guess I just wouldn't face it until I had to." She lapsed into silence while Aunt Jane concentrated on her driving. They had gone through several small towns and there was a state road west of Show Low she wanted to reach after they refueled.

Laurel again took the wheel as they left town while Aunt Jane watched road signs. Just east of Kohl's Ranch she found what she wanted and directed Laurel onto a narrow, winding road. It led across a bridge and up a rocky slope. At the top they parked the car to walk up the path, the fragrance of pine all around them. Ahead on a gentle slope stood a white frame two-story house, Zane Grey's lodge.

Laurel remembered reading his exciting western stories when she was younger. Dr. O'Hara had been an avid Zane Grey fan and their bookshelves were filled with his stories. Laurel had grown up literally surrounded by them.

It was thrilling to stand on the steps of the lodge he had built on the Mogollon Rim overlooking the great Tonto Basin. Here it was he had written books people the world over read and enjoyed. Here was the same big chair drawn up in front of the stone fireplace where the author had spent so many hours creating tales based on early Arizona history.

Laurel knew she would never forget this spot and loved Aunt Jane even more for bringing her here. She felt close to her father, wishing he could be with her.

Fighting to gain control, she blindly went out to the hewn log bench in front of the lodge. Oh, Dad, her heart cried out, why did we wait so long, and until it was too late? Why didn't we come here together? Why did we let life's "busyness" overshadow all the time we could have been sharing these special moments? Gradually the absolute stillness and peace of the pines calmed her, and once again she felt the rest only solitude can bring.

It was a long time before Aunt Jane came out. She knew Laurel needed time alone, and in her own unobtrusive way provided it. She brought a picture postcard for Laurel showing Zane Grey as a young man with his favorite horse, Night, a leading character in the best-selling novel *Riders of the Purple Sage.* Laurel clutched the bit of pasteboard, treasuring it for her scrapbook. That particular book had been her father's favorite.

They spent the night in a little town named Payson in the heart of the Tonto National Forest and were up early again the next morning. Aunt Jane was aglow with excitement. "Oak Creek Canyon today!" she announced. "It has to be the most beautiful spot in the world in autumn."

Several hours later Laurel had to agree. Never in her wildest dreams had she visualized a place like this! Giant red rocks reaching from valley floor as far as she could see to the blue sky above. Oak Creek itself, mysteriously winding, crossing, and recrossing, lost in its camouflage of willows. Switchbacks, arched tree branches making the road a cathedral. A lone horseman watering his pinto pony at a quiet pool, his dusty outfit etched against a gigantic overhang of rock.

"I don't believe what I'm seeing." Laurel gasped. "Rocks can't be those colors!" But they were. Scarlet, crimson, russet, orange, they ran the full gamut of red from deepest ruby to pale apricot. And the shapes! Boulders, pillars, castles, squares! Never had she seen such a place.

A strange hunger rose within her, a poignant longing for a way of life she had never known. She knew she would return, yet there was almost a gladness when they had climbed out of the canyon. Although that red rock citadel called her, it almost overpowered her. In spite of her reluctance to leave, she breathed a sigh of relief when they were within a few miles of Flagstaff.

Aunt Jane had said little on the trip up the canyon. Now she told Laurel that it had been her honeymoon trip. They had planned to come back, but things just hadn't worked out that way.

Laurel again marveled at the serenity of expression, and more so, at the love that could withstand so many years' separation without being dimmed. Just like my father, she remembered, and the thought warmed her. Again she found herself comparing. She was honest enough to admit her own feelings for Grant could never survive such a long time. They really hadn't gone beyond the excitement of the moment, the thrill of being selected and singled out by the young doctor so many nurses considered such a good catch. She smiled wryly. It hadn't taken long for the glamor to wear off once his mask slipped and she saw him as he was! The few days she and Aunt Jane had been gone seemed like ten years. Things that had been so vitally important such a short time ago had paled to insignificance in the new world she was discovering.

Would it be the same when it came time to seriously consider her father's letter? Laurel crowded the thought out of her mind. It wasn't fair to consider or even think about it until there was time to weigh every aspect. Just a few more days, she promised herself. Aunt Jane wants to spend at least a week at the Grand Canyon. There will be time then. Dad said not to rush into anything. Besides, a few more days can't matter after all these years.

Her train of thought was interrupted by Aunt Jane pointing out the city-limits sign of Flagstaff. A strange thrill went through her. If Many Tears hadn't interfered, this would have been her birthplace, hers and Willow's. Cloudy Willow probably wouldn't have died, and this strangely appealing town would have been as familiar to her as Phoenix now was.

Her thoughts raced on. She too would have been raised as an Indian princess of the tribe, the way Willow had been. Echo Cliffs, the Painted Desert, all would have been her home instead of the crowded city of Phoenix.

Lost in thought, Laurel waited while Aunt Jane made arrangements for lodging, then drove to a highly recommended restaurant specializing in Mexican food. Her heart beat rapidly each time she saw a dark-skinned girl in the long velvet skirts and silver jewelry many of them wore. She didn't realize the agitation showing in her face as she thought, These are my people too. Aunt Jane divined something of what she was feeling, and when they had been seated inside the candlelit restaurant and placed their order, she professed to be interested in some handcrafted silver in the lobby case. Excusing herself, she left Laurel alone in front of the great fireplace casting shadows across the dim room. As the leaping flames touched on her own tired face there was a muffled exclamation behind her, followed by the crash of a heavy chair. Her shoulders were gripped with iron hands and a man's voice furiously demanded, "Just what do you think you're doing? Why are you in Flagstaff?"

Chapter 5

For a moment Laurel was too stunned to move. Had Grant dared to follow her here? How could he?

Jerking herself free from the cruel grip, she whirled around to face him and looked straight into the eyes of a total stranger!

The tall, craggy-faced man in the khaki outfit gaped in amazement. His burning blue eyes met her own, now icy with anger! She was the first to recover and raised her head haughtily.

"I beg your pardon!" Her voice would have frozen a more courteous man, but the big oaf continued to stare. Rude, she thought scornfully, even as she noted the shock of sandy hair, suntanned face, and powerful shoulders.

The arrival of both Aunt Jane and their dinner broke the spell. "Someone you know?" she inquired.

Laurel looked directly into the stranger's face and replied bluntly, "I never saw this man before in my life."

With a grunt the stranger strode back to his table, flung down a bill, and marched out, leaving the chair overturned and his dinner half eaten.

"There goes a real man," Aunt Jane observed.

"Aunt Jane!" Laurel was shocked. "That rude creature!" In outraged tones she explained what had happened, finishing with, "I'll be lucky not to have bruises on my shoulders where the big brute grabbed me!"

Aunt Jane considered while she ate her enchiladas. Lowering her voice, she whispered, "He must have mistaken you for Willow."

"Oh, no!" Laurel dropped her fork in dismay. "I never thought of that. Oh, Aunt Jane, if I'd only known. I could have asked him about her!" She glared at the nearby table as though she could conjure him up again. Tears of disappointment filled her eyes.

"What a perfect opportunity, and I missed it."

Aunt Jane reached across the table to pat her hand.

"Maybe he doesn't even know her. It just seemed a logical explanation. Eat your dinner before it gets cold. Besides," she added, "until you decide for sure what you intend to do about the whole situation, it's probably just as well you didn't say anything."

"That's right," Laurel admitted, wiping her long lashes dry. "But I wonder what he meant if it was Willow he thought he recognized? 'Just what do you think you're doing? Why are you in Flagstaff?' I wonder how that would fit her any better than it fit me?"

Aunt Jane shook her head. "I don't know. Now go ahead and eat."

As usual Aunt Jane's common sense calmed Laurel down until she could thoroughly enjoy her tamale and taco dinner. She even followed Aunt Jane's lead and ordered sopapillas, those flaky pastry concoctions that are eaten with honey, and appreciated every morsel.

They left the restaurant and drove down the long main street. Laurel pulled the white Mustang to a stop in front of their motel, unaware of a dusty station wagon following at a discreet distance. An annoyed frown turned to a scowl as the driver watched the girl help the older woman carry suitcases into the cabin. He had been more shaken by the confrontation than Laurel.

A growing gleam of understanding lighted up his grim face, and he spoke aloud. "So that's it." Long after the lights had gone out he sat there, thinking. It wasn't until dawn touched the sky that he roused from his cramped position behind the wheel and drove away without a backward glance.

"How cold it is," Laurel commented as they started north a few hours later, teeth chattering in spite of a heavy coat and gloves.

Aunt Jane laughed. "It has every right to be, Laurel. Flagstaff is nearly seven-thousand feet elevation and Mr. Humphrey" — pointing to a peak faintly dusted with an unusually early snow — "is well over twelve-thousand feet. That's why there is so much color here. Their season is probably a month different than Phoenix."

Mid-September had touched the country with color. Where Oak Creek Canyon had run the spectrum of reds, the San Francisco Mountains displayed every hue of yellow and gold imaginable.

Laurel spoke truly when she exclaimed, "It's a King Midas world!" Clouds of golden aspen merged with clear yellow of white birch, silhouetted against the dark green Ponderosa pine and lacy juniper. They drove for miles in the fairyland of gold until in a little valley at the foot of the hills they came across a miniature church, the Chapel of the Holy Dove. Interdenominational, it was open at all times to travelers.

Laurel parked in front of it. There were

no others around — it was still quite early for traffic. Inside a split-rail fence, surrounded by trees, the oddly shaped building of rock and shakes stood. The steep-pitched roof was "for snow," Aunt Jane told her.

Stooping to enter the small door, Laurel found herself in a little room, bare except for a few short benches, a table with two candles, and a cross in the window that framed the distant mountain view. There were fresh golden flowers at the base of the cross showing that someone cared enough to keep it well tended.

Laurel stood transfixed. So much beauty in such a humble setting! Peace pervaded even the very air of the little room. With glistening eyes, she and Aunt Jane quietly closed the door. The next weary traveler would find the same atmosphere.

"I'm beginning to think I'm not even the same person you started out with," Laurel confided as they drove on.

Aunt Jane nodded understandingly.

Laurel went on. "Is it always like this? When you get away from the crowds and hustle and bustle of daily life? The people are different, too. I've never seen such friendly waitresses or motel owners, and the service-station attendants are so helpful."

Her voice altered. "I guess it would be impossible to live in such a land and be selfish or unkind. At least it would for me." She waved to the grandeur outside.

Again Aunt Jane contented herself with merely nodding. She could have told Laurel these things, but it was better for her to discover them for herself. Jane Scott had learned those same lessons many years ago. She loved this Arizona country in all its moods and seasons, especially the northern part. At first she had wondered how Laurel, city-bred sophisticate that she was, would react to the wild country, but she was thankful Laurel was able to see deeper than the obvious beauty of the land.

Aunt Jane smiled to herself. Laurel was coming through with colors as bright as the scenery outside! Today would be her supreme test, the Grand Canyon. Jane remembered her own first sight of the canyon and felt she should try and prepare Laurel a bit. Hesitantly she turned to the girl beside her.

"Laurel, in spite of all you've heard, seen, or read, you won't be prepared for the Grand Canyon." She fumbled for words. "No one can tell you what it's really like. It isn't a view, it's an . . . an experience."

Laurel looked at her in surprise. She had never heard such a thing. She had seen the pictures her vacationing friends brought home, mostly of various places with themselves posed in front of them, but the words of this simple gray-haired woman reached her as even the brilliant slides had not done.

Soberly she answered, "I'll remember, Aunt Jane."

The fragile moment was shattered by their arrival at Cameron Trading Post, where they turned west to the South Rim of the Grand Canyon. Laurel was enchanted by the stone buildings that looked like they had been there forever, and which were filled with souvenirs, both authentic and imported.

She would have bought out the store if it hadn't been for Aunt Jane. "There are many more places both at the canyon and elsewhere," she said.

Laurel laughed. Draped in silver and turquoise jewelry, she caught sight of herself in a mirror. Her eyes widened. "All I need is a beaded headband."

It was true. If Laurel's hair had been down and braided, for the first time she would have shown her mixed heritage and been what she really was, a blue-eyed Navajo. The thought rather pleased her, in startling contrast to her feelings a week before.

They walked down the little path to see the high bridge crossing the Little Colorado River but were disappointed to find a wide, dry streambed with only a trickle of muddy water in the red clay bottom. It was hard to believe that in flood the Little Colorado River could do immense damage.

A little way out of Cameron they saw their first Indian booths. Small, stall-like shelters with thatched roofs protected the brightly garbed sellers from the sun. Every kind of beadwork and blanket was for sale, and again Aunt Jane had to restrain her eager companion.

At last they arrived at Desert View, where they would get their first sight of the canyon. Desert View, with its circular red rock watchtower that could be seen for miles around from the air. Aunt Jane wouldn't let Laurel look over the rim until she led her away from a group near the guardrail.

"Now," she said gently, then stepped back, watching the girl rather than the view.

Wonder, incredulity, fear, delight, reverence. All were there, mirrored in Laurel's face. Satisfied, Aunt Jane retreated, leaving Laurel alone with her first view of the Grand Canyon.

She gripped the guardrail until her knuckles were white, Aunt Jane's words ringing in her mind.

". . . not a view . . . an experience." How right she had been! Before her lay a yawning gap in the earth of such magnitude her mind could not grasp it. Jumbles of rock — red, purple, streaked with creams and rust. Far below, a narrow ribbon she knew must be the mighty Colorado. As far as the eye could see, an awesome, beautiful, terrible chasm.

Vaguely she felt someone pause beside her, a wealthy man to judge by his clothing, polluting the air with a huge black cigar. Taking a casual look into the vista before him, he jerked the cigar out of his mouth, turned to his equally disinterested wife and muttered, "Huh! Some hole in the ground!" Then he jammed the cigar back in his mouth and marched off.

Never before had Laurel hated a perfect stranger as she did that unknown, insensitive man. For a moment Grant Carson's face swam before her. He probably would feel the same way, she thought. Unbidden came the Flagstaff stranger's face, stern, forbidding, strong. He would understand. Without considering, she knew it to be true. She forcibly brought her attention back to the canyon.

Laurel had heard stories of the canyon's pull, how for no apparent reason viewers suddenly leaped into the gaping wound in the earth as though drawn irresistibly. She had scoffed at the idea — heights held no fear for her — but now she was glad for the sturdy fence and guardrail to cling to.

Closing her eyes for a moment, she swallowed, then reopened them only to gasp in amazement. In the short moment she had looked away, the canyon's appearance had totally changed. Purple shadows had given way to reaching fingers of the afternoon sun. Other areas had grown dark, inaccessible to her gaze. She realized then the canyon was never the same. Each shifting shadow changed its mien.

No wonder the Indians fought for their land! she thought. I don't blame them. I would have too. I could never have let the white man take this from me.

She could bear no more at present and stumbled back to Aunt Jane. Silently they backed out and drove toward the South Rim, not speaking until they reached the Shrine of the Ages Chapel and American Legion Cemetery. Imposing rock pillars with a huge log cross marked the entrance. Idly they walked through, reading the stones of both great and small who were buried there. Laurel was also fascinated by the dioramas in the nearby Visitors' Center depicting the early expeditions. Vicariously she relived the hardships and rewards of their explorations, again torn by new yet familiar feelings.

It had been a small miracle they had been able to even get a room at the canyon. Aunt Jane had called the day they left Phoenix, pleading with the desk clerk at El Tovar that they would take "anything available." Finally he told them he did have a very small room with twin beds. Bright Angel Lodge was booked solid.

"It will be fine," they had reassured him cheerfully. Now they laughed across the small space between their beds and decided to bring in only what they needed each day, leaving the rest of their luggage in the Mustang.

Eyes sparkling, Laurel little resembled the woebegone girl who had sobbed her heart out days before. Aunt Jane was also relaxed. After walking to the Hopi House and browsing for a while, she announced her intention of taking a nap.

"Run along to the canyon, Laurel."

Laurel changed to a yellow sleeveless tunic and matching slacks, which Aunt Jane said made her look like an autumn leaf.

"Go to sleep." Laurel laughed and went out.

Avoiding the crowds, she found a small, deserted promontory with a big rock to lean against and gave herself up to the wonder of the canyon. If Desert View had been grand, the South Rim was spectacular. There was even greater scope and depth. She sat on an outcropping of rock that had stood since time began, it seemed. As her eyes adjusted she could see various vegetation on the canyon walls and discern tiny moving black spots on the trail following the canyon wall. It must be a mule trip returning from Phantom Ranch, the famed resort at the bottom of the canyon.

How tiny the people were, how infinitesimal against the mighty canyon! Yet each of them had hopes, dreams, fears, just like her.

Never before had Laurel considered the things she thought of that quiet afternoon. In spite of feeling dwarfed by the vastness around her, for the first time in her life Laurel also sensed her individual worth as a person, the importance each human life plays in the master game of eternity.

The long hours passed, drowsy, satisfying. Still she remained at the canyon's edge, lost in a sunlit world, renewing herself in the wonder of creation. Only when purple shadows blotted out the lingering sunset on the walls, leaving the canyon dark and indiscernible, did Laurel realize she was no longer alone. Aunt Jane had stolen near, sharing in the panorama and the strains of "Grand Canyon Suite" issuing from El Tovar, yet not intruding.

Laurel was shivering in her sleeveless outfit, glad for the soft yellow cardigan over Aunt Jane's arm. They weren't going to eat in the dining room, but walked down the path to the Bright Angel Lodge coffee shop.

"I'm too full of color to want a major dinner." Laurel laughed, and Aunt Jane agreed.

Coming back over the stone path near the rim, they peered into the mysteriously darkened canyon and laughed at the antics of the few daring squirrels still begging peanuts from the tourists when most of their companions had crept away to their burrows for the night. Aunt Jane sighed in pure contentment, and Laurel smiled.

"We can only stay a week?"

"Our room is only available for a week," Aunt Jane replied. "Besides, if we stay any longer the North Rim will be closed for winter. They get early snow — it's nine-thousand feet elevation up there." Laurel shivered with anticipation.

"I'm glad you had me pack warm clothes!"

The following week raced by, each day doubly precious because it brought them nearer to departure. Crisp mornings, golden days, snappy evenings. Short drives to different viewpoints. Ranger-Naturalist campfire talks. Indian dances and horseback rides. A trip to Phantom Ranch in the bottom of the canyon with Aunt Jane knowing every minute her mule was going over the edge! What a good sport she was!

But of all there was to do, Laurel loved best the lonely spot she had chosen for herself. Just off the rim walk from El Tovar to Bright Angel, the canyon itself held the most enjoyment for her. She spent hours there at different times of day, sometimes with Aunt Jane, more often alone. It almost became part of her personality. She could watch the clouds and predict when a thunderstorm was due, rushing inside at the last possible moment to avoid the elements. Forgotten were the troubles behind; those in the future were temporarily shelved.

In the quiet hours on the promontory she learned to totally accept the proud heritage of her mother's blood. A great love and yearning grew within her for the time when she would meet Willow, her long-lost sister. Yet she knew it was not yet time. She couldn't have told how she would know when it was the right time, only that she would know.

Dr. Grant Carson and his smallness receded into memory until she could smile to think what his reaction would be when people knew her background. She no longer felt any need to hide it. Those who loved her would love her still. What did it matter what others might think? Deep inside a dream began to grow, nebulous, still a dream. Would she someday take up her father's work at Vista d'Oro? Could the new doctor, what was his name again? Oh, yes, Dr. Cliff Barclay. Could he use her in the clinic? Much of course would depend on Willow's reaction. She still had to wait until she knew the time was ready and how to approach the entire situation.

The last afternoon at the South Rim once more found Laurel on her way to her special spot. As she approached, she was annoyed to hear children's voices. So far she had been undisturbed in her daily trysts. It would be a shame to have her last time spoiled, even though she loved children and missed her small charges from Ward 4 this last week.

Just before turning to her own viewpoint she heard a sharp scream. Dashing to the left she found a hysterical girl, perhaps ten, peering over the edge of the rim.

"Oh, dear God," Laurel whispered as her gaze followed the pointing finger. On a jutting shelf below lay a small boy, perhaps five or so, blood oozing from a jagged gash in his forehead. He had evidently slipped, then rolled until being knocked unconscious by a sharp rock.

Turning to the screaming girl, Laurel shook her violently to stop the hysterics. "Run for your parents," she ordered.

"B-b-but Billy." The girl's mouth quivered.

"Go!" Laurel repeated, the authority in her voice evident. The girl was off like a shot.

Laurel's training told her the blood from that head wound had to be stopped. He could bleed to death before help came. Gritting her teeth, she forced herself to start down the steep decline to the ledge. Refusing to look below into the canyon and certain death if she stumbled, she clutched the stubby brush and half slid to where Billy lay.

Taking the long white scarf from her head, she wadded it into a compress and pressed it directly on the wound, meanwhile feeling for his pulse. Thank God it was steady! She was relieved to see the cut wasn't as bad as she had

91

feared. The tiny bleeders just below the scalp always gave a head wound a misleading appearance. Now if the child would just stay unconscious until help came.

Shuddering, she looked down from their precarious perch. A struggling child on that narrow ledge could mean death for them both. Ten minutes seemed like eternity. Then the welcome face of a ranger appeared above.

"Everything all right down there?" He took in Laurel's appearance — bloodstains, torn slacks, dirty face.

"Fine," she called back, relief washing over her.

"We'll have you up in a minute," came back the reply.

Laurel could never have told afterward how she managed that trip. They sent down a small carrier litter for the boy, but she had to be hauled up with ropes. Bedraggled and shaking, she stepped out of the rope harness and into Aunt Jane's arms.

A camera snapped, and then again, an eager voice saying, "Boy, what a scoop! Why did you do it?" Too dazed to reply coherently Laurel could only murmur, "I had to, I'm a nurse," before reaction set in and she burst into tears, hating herself for doing so.

Aunt Jane led her through the gathering

crowd. "Make way, please. Yes, the doctor will come see her when he finishes with the little boy. I can take care of her until then."

It didn't take long for capable Aunt Jane to get Laurel cleaned up, and by the time the doctor arrived she was fast asleep. "When she awakens give her two of these," he said. "She's fine."

The doctor's prescription went begging. Laurel slept all night without once waking. Her first thought in the morning was of Billy.

"He's fine," Aunt Jane assured her. "He had five stitches and will be as good as new in a day or two. I hope his parents have sense enough to keep their children away from the canyon rim after this." Then, with a grim smile, she added, "There's a telegram for you."

Laurel frowned. "How can there be? No one knows where we are."

"Oh, yes, they do," Aunt Jane retorted. "Look at this." She held up a newspaper. Their faces looked out from the front page under blazing headlines:

DAUGHTER OF LEADING PHOENIX
SURGEON RISKS LIFE TO SAVE
LIFE OF SMALL CHILD
IN DARING FEAT OF BRAVERY

"Oh, no," Laurel exclaimed, noticing it was a Phoenix paper. "How did they get it so fast?"

"Wirephoto," Aunt Jane said. "Read the story."

Under the pictures of them and one of Billy with bandaged head and tearful eyes was a well-written story, praising Laurel's action. The reporter had chosen to close with appreciation of her courage and by quoting her. "When asked why she did it, Miss O'Hara modestly replied, 'I had to, I'm a nurse.' Some nurse is all we have to say."

Laurel thrust the paper aside. "Aunt Jane, we don't know who all will read that! We've got to get away, and fast!"

Aunt Jane's shrewd eyes looked straight at Laurel. "I've already thought of that, all you have to do is get dressed." She referred to the yellow telegram in Laurel's lap. "I kind of thought this might hurry things up."

Fearfully Laurel opened the message. It was brief and to the point.

AM ON MY WAY STOP WILL BE
THERE TOMORROW STOP
WAIT FOR ME AT EL TOVAR
DARLING

It was signed, "Grant."

Laurel was out of bed in a flash. Fifteen minutes later they had checked out, to the dismay of the desk clerk who wanted a forwarding address, and were once more on the road running away from young Dr. Carson.

Chapter 6

Grant Carson scowled furiously at the apologetic desk clerk.

"What do you mean, she isn't here?" he demanded. "I sent a telegram telling her I was coming today." He looked at the clerk suspiciously. "Wasn't it delivered?"

A wave of red mounted to the young clerk's hairline at the thinly disguised sneer but he replied steadily, "Yes, sir, as soon as it came in."

"Then I don't understand," the irate doctor went on. "I caught the first plane. How could she get away so fast? When did they leave?"

"Early this morning, sir, shortly after your telegram was delivered." The clerk's tone was even.

Dr. Carson jerked away from the counter, then turned back.

"Well, give me their forwarding address. Maybe I can catch up with them."

The clerk shook his head. "Sorry, sir, they left no address."

"No address! Just what kind of hotel are you running? Hotels always take forwarding addresses!"

The young desk clerk drew himself up haughtily. This had gone far enough. A crowd of other guests had begun to form and this obnoxious doctor certainly was making no effort to keep his voice down.

"I think you had better see the manager," he suggested icily, well knowing what kind of reception the manager would give him.

The following interview was highly unsatisfactory. Not only did the manager have no further information, he told the doctor plainly that hotel policy certainly didn't require guests to leave an address. When they paid their bill and left they were on their own. It was their business where they went, not El Tovar's.

With a muttered exclamation Dr. Carson slammed out. What should he do now? It was vitally important he contact Laurel immediately. Where could she have gone? He had been certain she was at Vista d'Oro, but earlier that morning when he had called Dr. Cliff Barclay, at last succeeding in rousing him from a much-deserved rest, he had no information either.

Yes, the telegram had arrived. It lay unopened on Dr. Barclay's desk. No, there was no Laurel O'Hara at Vista d'Oro. Willow O'Hara? There was no one there by that name, either. Now if Dr. Carson didn't mind, Dr. Barclay needed some sleep. He had a heavy schedule for the next day

Dr. Carson's dark eyes narrowed. Something awfully funny was going on. Had Dr. Barclay been lying? Was he really unable to give out any information, or just unwilling? He had sounded truthful, although sleepy, but Laurel must be there. Where else could she be?

The disgusted doctor walked to the edge of the canyon and casually glanced over. The beauty made no impression whatsoever on his bad mood. In fact, he rather resented the "pile of rocks" in front of him. What had got into Laurel? He had always found her pliable, willing to cooperate with his suggestions. He looked forward to molding her to his own ways once they were married. But this headstrong behavior! Leaving without a word. It had certainly put him in a spot. Everyone at the hospital had been asking about her. It was getting harder and harder to smilingly put up a front without letting on he didn't really know anything about her plans.

He thought of the thinly veiled sneer in Debi Thorne's questions about Laurel. The gorgeous redhead had hated Laurel since Dr. Carson had transferred his attentions to her. The uneasy man by the canyon rim squirmed. Frankly he preferred Debi, but it was Laurel who had the family background to help him get where he wanted. Why did life have to be so complicated?

The reason he had come here after seeing Laurel's picture in the paper, passed on to him by Debi, was because of the Desert General Board of Directors. They were planning a special ceremony in memory of Dr. O'Hara. Dr. Carson had told them Laurel would only be gone a few days, but when the days had stretched to a week, then ten days, they had grown impatient. His excuses were worn threadbare. He could see in the eyes of some of the most important men doubt of his own worthiness to eventually succeed Dr. O'Hara. They were rapidly losing faith in him.

Coming to a sudden decision, he rose and walked away without a backward glance. He had to find Laurel! The only thing to do now was go to Vista d'Oro himself and have it out with that Dr. Barclay. If Laurel wasn't there Dr. Barclay probably knew where she was and was covering up for her. One way or the other he had to get to the bottom of this affair and get Laurel back to Phoenix before the whole story broke wide open. If he could marry her before people found out her background, at least he could always say he hadn't known. By then he would probably be in at Desert General. He was sure they wouldn't do anything that would reflect on the memory of their beloved Dr. O'Hara. Yes, that's what he would do, find Laurel and marry her before they got back to Phoenix. He couldn't afford to lose this chance.

Leaving the Grand Canyon, he headed out to Cameron, totally ignoring the picturesque sellers along the roadside, and then turned left on U.S. 89, due north. What a horrible country! If the Grand Canyon had been the end of the earth, this was worse. Red dirt, low rises of ground, sagebrush, blue sky, emptiness. In the distance lay Echo Cliffs, red and forsaken-looking. Some of the crowd had been wanting to go to Page and take the Glen Canyon trip. If he went with them they would have to fly. He wouldn't drive this godforsaken land again for any trip!

The further north he drove the angrier he became with Laurel, the unknown Dr. Barclay, and life in general. There wasn't even a decent service station by his standards. Well, he had enough gas to get to this Vista d'Oro. Surely they would be a little more civilized if there was a white doctor there. Hadn't the letter mentioned some kind of missionary, also? Anything would be better than these tiny cluttered buildings along the way, he thought disparagingly.

His lip curled in contempt for Dr. Barclay. How could any doctor in his right mind deliberately choose to live out here? No one could be expected to come to such a place. The Oath of Hippocrates he had taken meant little to Dr. Carson. He scorned the idealists and dreamers who used medicine to make the world a little better place to live in; his interest was the prestige and wealth that could be accumulated if the right strings were pulled.

On second thought, he decided, I'm glad it is like this. Laurel will be glad enough to leave this place as fast as we can get out of here. The thought cheered him, and it was almost with anticipation he took the road leading from the main highway to Vista d'Oro. It was a good thing he had been watching for it. The road sign was faded, hard to read.

The winding road was of hard-packed earth and led up and around, across the flat land to sloping mesas and rock walls ahead. At the top of a rather steep incline he could see a tiny patch of green far ahead. That must be Vista d'Oro. Forgetting how misleading the clear desert air can be, he gauged it to be just a few miles away. He speeded up, only to frown as the motor of his yellow sports car sputtered a few times then with a final cough stopped. He glanced at the gas gauge. Empty! If that wasn't the last straw. Now what was he to do?

He waited a little while, then realized there had been no sign of life whatsoever since he had left the main highway. Not even a jackrabbit was in sight. Stories of stranded travelers came to mind. What was it they said? Was it better to stay with the car or try and walk? Judging from the distance he had come, it couldn't be over ten miles more into town. Ten miles! How could he walk that far? His thin shoes weren't made for walking anywhere, let alone on this rough road. But what else could he do? It was getting hotter and hotter in the car.

Seething inside, he slowly stepped from the car and started up the road. This was all Laurel's fault. If she hadn't run away, it would never have happened. He visualized Debi Thorne's face if she could see him now. It only increased his anger as he started walking up the long, hot, dusty road to Vista d'Oro, promising himself Laurel would pay for this.

Dr. Cliff Barclay was tired, bone tired.

First the long day yesterday, then the annoying telephone call from that city doctor. A scornful look crossed his rugged countenance. Dr. Grant Carson sounded like one of those sleek city opportunists, the kind Dr. Barclay despised. Making their living by humoring rich patients. Oh, yes, Dr. Barclay knew of Mountainside. A private hospital, reserved for the mighty. That was one of the things he had been glad to leave behind when he discovered Vista d'Oro. He hated the socializing many doctors felt necessary to further their careers. A man should be able to get ahead by hard work rather than by the whims of rich patrons. He smiled wryly to himself. No need to worry, he would never lose his position to an ambitious young doctor. Vista d'Oro was beyond the pale as far as most of them would be concerned.

Dr. Barclay's eyes softened as he surveyed the spotless clinic. Dr. O'Hara's original building had been expanded. In addition to a combination waiting room/office, there was an examining room, a small but well-equipped surgery, and an eight-bed ward. There were also two tiny cubicles that could serve as "private rooms" when needed. All ten beds had been needed when measles hit the village six months ago. Every bed had been full. He rather suspected it was the status of being in the "hospital" rather than the sickness itself that had kept the beds filled. One good thing had come out of it — those parents whose children hadn't caught it had finally accepted the shots he had been trying to promote in the two years he had been at Vista d'Oro.

The look of softness vanished. He needed help. The two Navajo girls who cleaned and served as receptionists did a good job, but he needed help with actual treatments. His only fully trained helper, Mrs. Molly, was a jewel. When she had retired due to age from the Flagstaff hospital, her daughter and son-in-law insisted she live with them "so Mother could rest."

Dr. Barclay chuckled, remembering the irate woman who had come to see if he could use her at Vista d'Oro. He had never seen anyone less likely to settle down and do nothing. She wanted work, and how she found it! Her duties went far beyond her L.P.N. training, but what else could he do? She assisted with everything he did, from surgery to stitching up cuts when a teary-eyed child brought in a puppy or kitten.

Yes, Mrs. Molly was priceless. When she did have a minute off, she baked cookies for the children and visited the aged. She was totally selfless, limited only by enough hours in the day for what she wanted to accomplish. What he really needed was an R.N. She could relieve both him and Mrs. Molly.

He also needed a housekeeper. He had put his foot down regarding Mrs Molly taking care of his home in addition to everything else. As a result, it was a mess. He didn't have time to do it. Sighing, he shook his head.

Then there was Willow. She had the natural feelings and intelligence to make an outstanding nurse. She had helped as much as she knew how, but neither he nor Mrs. Molly had time to really train her. He wished she could take training, but she hadn't consented. It was strange she had remained unmarried. She was a beautiful girl. But lately there had been something about her that troubled him. She seemed restless, sad.

Could she possibly have guessed? No, he told himself vehemently, I was the only one Many Tears told. He thought of her blue eyes that should have identified her heritage even before Many Tears's story. I had been too busy to even worry over it, he guessed.

How can I get an R.N.? His mind returned to the knotty problem.

Where would he find a capable woman who would be willing to come to the desert and live in such a simple manner? Just because he loved the work and the people didn't mean others would. Yet, his mind persisted, Peter Thompson does.

Peter! Dr. Barclay's heart warmed. When the young missionary had come to Vista d'Oro, "Dr. Cliff," as the Navajos affectionately called him, had held his breath and wondered. He liked the missionary on sight. Yet would the man be able to understand and appreciate Navajo traditions? Would he tear them down in order to preach his own creed? Would he be able to relate them to his own beliefs, or would he give up in despair as so many others had done?

He needn't have worried. Peter Thompson saw the great beauty of the people's beliefs. He never downgraded or attempted to lessen the teachings of their forefathers. Instead, he blended them in, adding to what they already had, teaching a richer and better way of life. Cliff and Peter had become fast friends. What little free time they had off they spent together, and because of their own individual callings, often found themselves working together.

Dr. Barclay wondered if Willow knew Peter Thompson was in love with her. He had been from the first Sunday morning when he invited all who cared to come to meet in the little schoolhouse for a service. Willow had been among the first, beautiful in her native clothing.

Perhaps that was what was bothering Willow. Her face flashed to mind, then, closely following, the face of the girl in Flagstaff. That had been a strange experience. Willow had asked the day before if she could go with him — she needed materials and things.

"I'm sorry, Willow," he told her, genuinely regretful. "I'll be too busy to look after you. You can go next time." He hadn't added he didn't like the way some of the Flagstaff street loungers watched her.

She had been a little resentful, and finally flared up. "All right. I'll get there by myself. I don't have to wait for you." Half concerned that she might keep her promise, when he saw her in the dim restaurant light his temper rose. Even though it really wasn't any of his business, he had tried to keep an eye on Willow after Many Tears died. She seemed so alone, in spite of being surrounded by others. Striding to her he demanded, "Just what do you think you're doing? Why are you in Flagstaff?"

When she turned and shot back, "I beg

your pardon!" he was amazed. It was Willow, yet it wasn't. With all her dignity, Willow couldn't have carried off that scene. Then, too, there was the white woman with her. Willow was pretty shy of strangers.

"I never saw this man before in my life." The Flagstaff girl's voice rang in his ears. After staring to make sure Willow wasn't getting even for leaving her in Vista d'Oro, he had stamped out. In the dusty clinic station wagon with time to think, Many Tears's story came back. Was this the sister then? What was her name, Laurel? Discreetly he followed and watched them, then in the early-morning hours drove home. Willow was still a little sulky when she came in that morning, but she couldn't have been in Flagstaff. When the telegram came addressed to Laurel, he was convinced Willow's twin had been in the city that evening.

Dr. Cliff felt torn inside. Had Dr. O'Hara revealed Laurel's parentage to her before he died? Did she know of Vista d'Oro and of Willow? Was she coming here? That's all I need, he thought, for her to show up and upset Willow. Or would it?

It was too big for him. Maybe the girl was just sightseeing with no knowledge or intention of invading his territory. He sincerely hoped so. He ignored the tiny voices inside whispering, Do you?

With a harsh laugh he rose and leaned against the door frame. Time to lock the clinic and get some dinner before the evening patients started coming. He was tired. What he needed was not more problems, but an R.N. The sixty-four-dollar question was where to get one, and how.

His attention was caught by a moving dot on the road coming into the village. As it came closer he saw it was a man, but who? No one from Vista d'Oro would be out now. It was dinnertime. All of his people would be home. As the man reached the small gate in front of the clinic, Dr. Cliff saw it was a total stranger. The thin shoes were sliding on the rough road, perspiration streaked his face. His once-immaculate shirt and slacks were covered with dust.

Dr. Cliff was beside him instantly.

"Water," he gasped, leaning heavily on the doctor, who led him into the clinic. In the waiting room the stranger's legs gave way, and he dropped heavily into a chair.

Grabbing the glass from Dr. Cliff he drank heavily in great gulps until Dr. Cliff took it from him, saying, "It will make you sick to drink too much at once." He added, "What happened to you?"

"Ran out of gas," the stranger tersely replied. Then with a blaze of hate showing through the dirt and grime, he continued, "I came for Laurel."

Astonishment held Dr. Cliff frozen, then he regained his composure. "Laurel?"

"Yes, Laurel," the stranger snapped. "I am her fiance, Dr. Grant Carson."

"I see," Dr. Cliff replied quietly, with a strange, sinking feeling inside. "Then you are the man I talked with earlier today. I told you she wasn't here."

"I know what you told me." Dr. Carson sneered. "But I also know she was at the Grand Canyon early this morning. Look." He held out the Phoenix paper with Laurel and Aunt Jane's picture on the front.

Slowly Dr. Cliff read the story, admiration for the act evident in his face. It seemed to infuriate his visitor even more.

"You can't tell me she isn't coming here. When I read that letter you wrote to her father I knew it would only bring trouble. What right did you have to meddle anyway? What business was it of yours?"

Dr. Cliff looked at him steadily. "The business of any doctor who makes a promise to his dying patient."

Dr. Carson had the grace to look ashamed, but not for long. "If you will kindly direct me to a hotel, I'll get a room.

She should be here tomorrow at the latest."

Dr. Cliff laughed outright. "Hotel? There's no such thing in Vista d'Oro. This isn't a tourist center, Dr. Carson. This is a village."

A look of blank dismay swept over Dr. Carson's face. "Then where can I stay?"

You should have stayed in Phoenix, Dr. Cliff thought, but refrained from speaking it aloud.

"My friend Peter Thompson, the missionary, has a spare bedroom. Maybe he'd let you use it overnight."

"Can you call him?" Dr. Carson demanded.

"Certainly." Dr. Cliff's eyes twinkled as he stepped to the doorway and shouted, "Hey, Pete! Can you come over for a minute?

"We don't have telephones except for the clinic and my home," he smoothly explained.

Dumb with surprise, silenced for once in his life, Dr. Carson sat meekly until a man in his mid-twenties entered. Although tall, he appeared dwarfed by the doctor's brawn. Cool gray eyes under wavy brown hair showed compassion, and the line of his mouth denoted an unusual strength in one so young.

Unsmiling, Dr. Cliff explained the stranger's plight, carefully omitting his reason for coming. After another cool, measuring glance, Peter motioned Dr. Carson ahead of him across the path to his small cottage. Dr. Cliff stood in the doorway, wondering what all this might mean. He dreaded the ripples this stranger's visit might cause in the peaceful pool of Vista d'Oro daily life. Yet in spite of himself a thrill shot through him. Could it be possible Laurel O'Hara was coming here? And she was an R.N.

Rudely shoving the thought aside, he went home, ate a light meal, held his evening office hours, and finally locked the clinic for the night. But his gaze lingered long on the side of Peter Thompson's house where the spare bedroom lay, now occupied by the unwelcome guest.

In that same spare bedroom Dr. Carson disdainfully looked around. Rough furniture, handmade, he thought. Coarse blankets. Cheap curtains. At least it was clean, and the meal he had shared with Peter Thompson had been tasty, though plain food. What a place! Only the bare necessities! The thought brought a satisfied smile to his face in spite of his sore feet and foul mood. If this was a sample of Vista d'Oro homes, and at least from the outside it had appeared above average, Laurel, used to every luxury, was in for a rude awakening.

He pulled the cotton, highly starched curtain aside and glared at the clinic. It galled him to have to accept a favor either from Dr. Barclay or his friend Peter Thompson. Dr. Carson despised "do-gooders." That's what both of them are, he told himself viciously after climbing into the hard bed. Do-gooders, both of them. Yet in spite of his arrogance and although he would never have admitted it, deep inside he knew both Dr. Barclay and Peter Thompson were twice the man he was, and he hated them for it.

Chapter 7

Willow O'Hara stood at her bedroom window, watching the sun rise. She had been there quite some time. First the sky lightened, then a soft glow appeared. At last the full glory of the brilliant orb burst over the horizon, touching the desert with light.

It wasn't the first sunrise she had watched from her window. Somehow the rising sun called her. It was such a quiet time of day, a time for hopes and dreams. But this morning tears filled her eyes, and she didn't know why.

I'm so alone, she thought. A longing filled her for something she had never known. She looked around the cosy room Mrs. Molly had fixed for her after Many Tears had died. Mrs. Molly was a dear. The little room facing the rising sun was filled with small comforts. Indian blankets, treasures from Willow's childhood, they were all there. Her gaze rested on the open closet door. Velvet Indian skirts side by side with white uniforms she wore to the clinic.

The clinic! Thought of it brought to mind Dr. Cliff. Willow's head dropped to the windowsill. She was sorry for the way she had acted about going to Flagstaff. Dr. Cliff had been good to her. She hadn't been able to explain to him the sudden urge to get away from Vista d'Oro she had felt. She hadn't even been able to understand it herself.

Maybe she should go away and take nurse's training as he advised. She loved her work at the clinic but was limited in what she could do. Both Dr. Cliff and Mrs. Molly said she could become a wonderful nurse. Part of her longed for the chance and wanted to go. Yet there was a secret fear within that held her back from applying.

Determined to face what was bothering her, Willow resolutely made herself think back. She knew it had something to do with the white men she would be forced to meet if she left Vista d'Oro. Forcing herself to remember, she lived over her childhood years. How long ago they seemed!

Willow had been about seven when she first knew she was different from the other village children. Until then she had attended school and played with the others. Then one day a party of rough traders had come looking for handicrafts to sell in their trading post. Willow had been standing round-eyed.

One crude fellow remarked to his comrade, "Hey, look! Look at the blue-eyed Navajo!" and laughed meaningfully.

Willow hadn't known what they meant but rushed to Many Tears and demanded, "What is it? What do they mean?"

Many Tears replied simply, "Your father had blue eyes."

Her answer satisfied the child Willow, but the girl Willow recalled them many times, puzzling over what they meant. Her questions to Many Tears and others of the village brought no response. It seemed the whole adult village knew of a mystery about Willow's blue eyes, but no one would tell her. In time she ceased to ask. She grew to feel her father must have been very wicked. No one in the village ever spoke his name.

Perhaps it was those feelings that had caused Willow to hold back from the other village young people. The other girls were jealous of Willow and resented her beauty. She found the only way to combat their remarks was to stay away from village social life. Before long she had earned the reputation of being a lone wolf and was left to herself. No one knew the times she had cried herself to sleep in sheer loneliness, hating the fact she was "different" from the others. Yet there wasn't a young man for miles around who didn't secretly admire her tall slenderness, shining dark hair, and those wonderful blue eyes. There wasn't a girl in the village who wouldn't have given her best silver jewelry to look like Willow.

When she started work at the clinic and came to live with Mrs. Molly, the void of emptiness had been filled for a while, but now she sat by the window, filled with deep longing to really belong to someone. If she went for training would she be accepted and find friends, or would she only be "the blue-eyed Navajo" in a strange world? She shrank from the idea as she had once run from the man who called her that.

Willow's attention was caught by the door of the mission softly opening. Peter Thompson stepped out, stretching in the sunlight, facing the morning sky. The watching girl drew back behind her protecting curtain as he looked toward Mrs. Molly's house and her room, unaware she was watching. A look of longing was in his face. Willow's face reflected the rosy rays of the sun. She was aware of the young missionary's growing admiration. His soft gray eyes gave him away although he tried to hide it. She was also aware of how much she had learned to care for him. Softness filled her eyes, quickly replaced by a flood of tears. Misery filled her. How could she accept this man's love? Her unknown background hovered above her like a blanket, shrouding the joy she could know.

"Great Spirit, Peter's God," she prayed. "Who was my father? Why will no one speak his name? Was he an outcast?" Then after a long silence she whispered, "And who am I?"

The wave of misery receded, leaving her white and pale. Determination filled her as she watched Peter cross to Dr. Cliff's house by the clinic. She loved this man too much to bring shame to him. Yet how could she go on, seeing him daily, without betraying herself?

I will go away, she thought dully. When spring comes I will go to nurse's training as Dr. Cliff and Mrs. Molly want me to do. While I am gone, surely he will forget me. A fresh pang shot through her but she put it aside. She could hear Mrs. Molly stirring. She must not see Willow's tears. Hastily donning her uniform and washing her face, she hurried to the kitchen, forcing a pleasant greeting as she helped prepare their simple breakfast.

Willow had no way of knowing that Mrs. Molly's sharp gaze saw right through her. She was a wise woman, wise enough not to ask questions. It was better for Willow to come to her when she was ready. Instead of prying, Mrs. Molly turned the breakfast talk to the day's duties, intertwining amusing incidents of the village children. She was rewarded by Willow's quiet laughter and some of her sparkle returning. By the time they left for the clinic Willow had firmly put her troubles aside. There was no place for them in her work. It demanded every bit of skill and attention she had to give.

This morning was no exception. One of the village mothers who was long overdue with her baby waited on the steps, face glistening with labor pains. Dr. Cliff was just unlocking the door and scolding, "Why didn't you wake me?" The woman only shook her head, glad to get inside.

It didn't take long to prepare her. Willow helped Mrs. Molly, then hurried to make sure everything was ready for the coming baby. Twenty minutes later a thin cry filled the air, thrilling Willow. That first cry of life never failed to rouse within her a longing for the day when she too would hold a little one in her arms. The thought made her gentle as she capably cleaned and wrapped the tiny body, then placed it in the mother's waiting arms.

"A boy." She smiled, knowing how happy

the parents would be. Their first two children had been girls. The mite nestled against his mother contentedly. Willow was glad Dr. Cliff believed the mother and baby should be together.

A little later the proud father was allowed to visit. "For my son." He pointed out the window. Willow carefully avoided looking at Dr. Cliff or Mrs. Molly, concentrating instead on the mother's face.

She echoed, "For our son," and Willow noted she saw no incongruity that her husband had brought a newly purchased pinto pony for an hour-old baby. In spite of Willow's desire to laugh she felt a mist in her eyes at the look passing between mother and father. Had her own father ever looked at her mother like that?

Glancing up, she caught a strange look on Dr. Cliff's face. He masked it quickly, saying, "Well, what next?" and shrugging. Their work was not by appointment, but by necessity.

It proved to be a full day. A man with a broken arm and a rider whose horse had kicked him were only two of the patients who came in. By late afternoon Willow was exhausted.

Seeing her tired look Dr. Cliff had told her, "Finish what you're doing, Willow, then go on home. Get out in the fresh air. It will do you good."

Gratefully she thanked him and a little later slowly walked to Mrs. Molly's house. Dr. Cliff saw her go, his brow furrowed. Something was on her mind, he was sure of that. Maybe he should have a talk with her. Yet how could he? Until he knew what was to happen regarding Laurel, his hands were helplessly tied. He had been thankful Dr. Grant Carson had not appeared near the clinic today. The last thing he wanted was for that snob to get anywhere near Willow.

"No," he said aloud. "She will have to work it out for herself."

"I agree." Mrs. Molly had come up behind him. "She will, too. She has inner strength that has never been tested. I'd be willing to bet whatever comes that girl will come through flying banners of courage."

Dr. Cliff gave the plump shoulders a squeeze. "Thanks Mrs. Molly, I needed that." Together they watched Willow start down the path leading to the mesa above town. She had changed to walking shoes but still wore her white uniform. Gone was the tired droop. She walked erect, proudly, her face lifted to the hill above.

Dr. Cliff smiled at Mrs. Molly. "Well, end of break. Better get back to work."

"Yes," she agreed. "I have to get some dinner for our little mother. I'll throw in enough for you."

Dr. Cliff frowned. "If we could just get you some help!"

"What about you?" Mrs. Molly replied with a pert tilt to her nose. "Don't think you can outwork me, do you?"

He laughed. "No, Mrs. Molly, but we both need help, that's for sure." With a last look at Willow, now a white spot etched against the mesa, they wearily trudged back to their duties, hoping no one else would come in for a while.

Willow stepped lightly and surely as she followed the familiar upward path to the mesa. It was her favorite climb. A great pinyon tree stood on top, providing a natural bench. Behind her lay Echo Cliffs, mellowed by the late-afternoon sun. Before her the ground sloped to the country leading to the Painted Desert. Great rocks raised their bulk to the sky, and lazy birds of prey drifted against the blue sky.

Since she was a child Willow had loved this place without knowing why. It called her, even as the sunrise did, promising peace and quiet. It seemed far away from Vista d'Oro, which lay in the valley below. Yet today even the stark beauty of the mesa could not completely erase Willow's loneliness. Usually it was enough just to sit looking out over the panoramic view that gave the village its name, but today unrest filled her. Never had it been so breathtaking. Was it because she had decided to leave it all? Could she leave it? Could she trade this strange, wild life for city streets? Mrs. Molly said it took a year to become an L.P.N., longer to become an R.N., which was what Dr. Cliff wanted Willow to be. Could she spend a whole year, let alone two, away from this golden land? Vista d'Oro. The name itself spread warmth through her.

"I just can't do it," she cried out to the slowly setting sun. "This is my land. These are my people." She didn't dream that over twenty years ago her father had stood on this spot, saying the same words. If she only could have known!

Are they your people? The slight breeze that had risen mocked her. How could Many Tears have had a blue-eyed child? There were no blue-eyed Navajos unless . . . Willow shuddered at the thought. She had heard stories of white men who promised trusting Indian girls marriage. Had Many Tears been betrayed? Yet she must have been old when Willow was born. How could such a thing be?

"If I only knew!" The girl threw herself to the ground, beating her fists against the fragrant carpet of needles beneath her.

On the trail below Dr. Grant Carson heard the sound. Triumph filled him. It wouldn't be long now.

He had spent a rotten day. Forced to accept Peter Thompson's hospitality, he had moped around the village, peering into open doorways, asking questions.

The Navajos ignored him. He didn't know if they couldn't speak enough English to understand him or whether they were feigning ignorance. He had never been interested enough to learn anything about the Indian people. Oddly enough now, he felt uncomfortable in their presence. Their expressionless faces as they listened to his questions and went on with their work put him at a strange disadvantage.

In disgust he attempted to quiz Peter Thompson but found him aloof. His host was courteous, even taking gas to rescue the yellow sports car, but didn't talk much.

Sullen fellow, Dr. Carson decided. He would have been surprised to see the antics Peter joined in with the children of the village when there was time. They loved him.

Dr. Carson complained about everything. He sneered at the meager amounts of water available when Peter told him there was none for him to wash his car. Peter patiently explained that it had been extremely dry that summer and fall, but as soon as the rains came the wells would be full.

"I won't be here then," Dr. Carson haughtily told the missionary.

Thank the Lord for that, Peter thought, a boyish grin escaping in spite of himself. Seeing the look Dr. Carson hastily changed the subject.

"There's a girl here, Willow O'Hara," he stated. "I'd like to see her."

"Willow O'Hara?" the missionary looked directly at his guest. "I know of no one here by that name."

Dr. Carson found himself up against the same blank wall he had encountered with Dr. Cliff. His resentment boiled over.

"Don't know or won't tell me?" he raged, completely losing control of himself. "Everyone here can't be that innocent! Something funny is going on and I mean to get to the bottom of it! In spite of all your supposed lack of knowledge I'm staying here until I get what I came for!"

Peter Thompson raised his hand. "Then you'd better change your attitude, Dr.

Carson. The room you are now in is the only thing in the village that would be available to you. You can use it as long as you like. But I refuse to be spoken to in my home" — he stressed the word home — "as you have been attempting to do. If you plan to stay, you will keep a civil tongue in your head." He looked unflinchingly into Dr. Carson's startled eyes. The doctor's gaze fell first.

"I'm sorry," he mumbled, half defiantly. "It's just that I'm so worried about Laurel . . ."

"Laurel?" Peter interrupted. "I thought you said you were looking for a Willow?"

"Her twin sister." The words poured out. Peter Thompson had to believe the strange story Dr. Carson told. It was too incredible to be anything but true. Did Willow know this? Loving her as he did, he thought not. He had seen the hurt at sly digs of the village maidens. Somehow the truth left her even more defenseless. He sat silently as Dr. Carson continued with the story. He told of the letter, of his own last interview with Laurel.

"I think she was a little upset by my frankness, but you understand my position, I am sure," he finished.

Without speaking Peter rose and walked

out. His hands were clenched beside him. His parting look would have shriveled a more sensitive man than Dr. Carson. Never in years had Peter Thompson been so angry. He wanted to strike out at this bigoted doctor who dared pursue a girl such as this Laurel must be! And Willow, what of her? What would this story mean in her life, and in his own? He cared little for her parentage, he never had. But if she were the daughter of an eminent surgeon did he have a right to proclaim his love? When she knew would she be willing to stay in Vista d'Oro? It was unthinkable that he leave. He had learned to love both the town and Dr. Cliff. He was needed here, his work in life shaped the mold that brought him to this tiny village in the middle of nowhere. He had thought it perfect to find a mate here who could share with him the work among her own people. Now everything was changed.

Peter shuddered at the storm that was gathering over the previously peaceful village. So many lives touched by the theft of a child by a heartbroken old woman! Turning instinctively to the mission chapel, he entered its cool quietness. He needed strength before he could decide what to do. He had to see Dr. Cliff and confirm the story. Then Willow must be told. But how, and by whom? Blindly he knelt, too stunned to pray, and let the stillness sink into his soul and prepare him for what might lie ahead.

Back in his cottage Dr. Carson stared as the door closed behind the missionary. He really hadn't meant to blurt out the whole story. He could see Peter Thompson's reaction wasn't good at all. If Laurel were here, it might put her on guard, although he had begun to believe perhaps she wasn't. Uneasily he stood and looked from the window. On the path leading to the mesa he spotted a dark-haired girl in a white uniform. Laurel! A spurt of hope shot up. She was here! They had all lied to him!

He burst through the door, calling her name, but she was too far ahead to hear. He tried to run but his leather shoes slid beneath him. Blast this hard ground! Oh, well, there was only one path. He would follow it until he found her.

It was a long hot climb to the mesa top. He was drenched with perspiration. The sun had nearly set by the time he paused on the trail, wondering if she could possibly have turned off. The sob from above sparked hope. He tried to walk more rapidly, but his tired muscles refused to cooperate. They worked well on a smooth green golf course, but here on this desert mesa, they were no match for the terrain. It was another fifteen minutes before he gained the top.

There she was! Dr. Carson exulted. Face down under the tree, crying her heart out. In the face of such grief he paused. He had never seen Laurel like this, even when her father died. That was one of the things he admired most, her self-control. For a moment his heart was touched. Poor little girl! This whole thing had been a terrible shock to her system. He would get her away from here as fast as he could and never again would she have to think of Vista d'Oro or her father's letter. She would be only too glad to follow his suggestions about keeping her parentage secret.

Confidently he walked toward her, his steps silenced by the thick, springy mat beneath his feet. With an unusual show of tenderness he gathered her into his arms and bent to kiss her. He was stopped by a piercing cry, a ringing slap across the face, followed by many painful little blows. Half blinded with pain and anger he released her and she sprang back, fury in every muscle, disheveled and tear-stained, yet more beautiful than he had ever seen her.

Dumbfounded he stared, shaking his head in bewilderment, trying to think clearly. This wildcat was not Laurel. His mind reeled. The magnificent beauty before him must be the long-lost twin, Willow O'Hara!

Chapter 8

It must have been a full minute they stood there, the beautiful girl at bay, the doctor flabbergasted. The girl regained her poise first.

"Who are you and why did you follow me?" she asked.

The doctor, more shaken than he cared to admit, blurted out the last thing in the world he had planned to say at that moment.

"I thought you were your sister." If he hadn't been so confused he would have been more discreet. A look of amazement followed by disbelief crossed Willow's face before she mimicked him.

"My sister!" She laughed scornfully, the biting edge of her sarcasm cutting through his veneer of sophistication. An unbecoming red mounted his smooth-shaven face, giving him the guilty look of someone caught red-handed.

"It's true," he muttered, not knowing how to respond without saying too much.

Willow's clear laugh rang out again. She knew this man was caught in his own trap. "I have no sister," she told him. "Everyone in the village knows that!"

Her disbelief was too much for the arrogant Dr. Carson. Suddenly he wanted to humiliate her the way he had been humiliated. If he couldn't hurt Laurel then he could put this high and mighty girl in her place. Gripped in the fury of his own passion he seized Willow by the shoulders, forcing her to face him squarely.

"Yes, you do have a sister," he told her mercilessly. "A twin sister, Laurel, who is even now on her way to find you. Don't pretend you didn't know all about her. What did you think you'd gain by acting? I know these things are true, I am Laurel's fiance. Your father —" He stopped for breath as Willow gasped. She couldn't help believing him now and stood petrified in his grip as he went on.

"Your father was Dr. Mike O'Hara, who built this clinic. Your mother was Cloudy Willow, who died giving birth to you and Laurel. The woman you thought was your mother was really your grandmother, Many Tears. She's responsible for all this! She stole you when you were born, then had an attack of conscience just before she died and told your precious Dr. Cliff Barclay the whole story. He wrote to Dr. O'Hara, and Dr. O'Hara left a letter for Laurel to read after he died."

Shaking her to emphasize his point, he rushed on, maddened by the indignities he had suffered because of these people.

"You think you will be able to live up to your sister Laurel?" There was hate in his voice. "Never! She has been raised in a white man's world, you have been raised here." He waved one hand toward the shadowy desert with its afterglow of color. "You can never fit into her world. When she comes the best thing you could do would be tell her to leave you alone! She will go back to her own people and you can stay here where you belong!"

Suddenly he realized the face before him had gone pale as death. His hold loosened. For a moment the girl swayed, then quick as a flash she was running down the steep trail. Fear for her safety pierced through his anger and he started after her. "Wait, Willow! Wait!"

Ahead of him on the trail Willow could hear his feet pounding. He was heavier than she and even with slick-soled shoes on the downhill path could overtake her. In panic she increased her speed, then, rounding a path, slipped on a loose rock and fell heavily. She clutched at the stunted brush, but the fall had set her in motion and slowly she slipped over the edge of the trail, down,

down into the valley below. It was a gentle slope or she could never have stopped herself. When she did, she was bruised and bleeding. Her hands were raw, hurt, but not so hurt as her heart. She couldn't think of the things he had told her now. They were too new, fresh. She heard the stranger stop at the top of where she had fallen and lay motionless. Maybe he would go away, thinking he had killed her. It really didn't matter, she thought, as a piercing pain shot through her left ankle. When she thought the stranger had gone, she tried to stand. The pain was too much, and for the first time in her life Willow fainted, dropping into a pitiful heap by the side of a big clump of sagebrush.

On the trail above Dr. Carson peered over, trying to see where she was. He had seen her go over the edge. He knew in his heart it was his fault. He was to blame for the accident, because he had been unable to control his temper.

He called her name, over and over, but there was no answer. At last he realized she either wouldn't or couldn't reply. As fast as he could he made his way back to town bursting into the clinic.

"Come quick, Dr. Barclay, Willow has fallen."

It was characteristic of Dr. Cliff that he asked no unnecessary questions. "Where?" he demanded, and as Dr. Carson, breathing hard, tried to explain, he told him, "You'd better show me."

Setting off in the twilight, they soon came to the spot where Willow had slipped. Giving Dr. Carson a strange look, Dr. Cliff carefully made his way to where Willow lay and picked her up as he would a child. He took care to see her hurt ankle was held as well as it could be.

Dr. Carson followed rather helplessly. "Can I do anything?" He sounded humble.

Dr. Cliff looked straight at him for a moment, then replied curtly, "I rather think you've done enough. I don't know what it was you said to Willow on the mesa. I do know that she would never run down that path unless she was half scared to death. There are a lot of questions I'm going to be asking you when I get her taken care of, and believe me, Dr. Carson, you'd better have some good answers!"

Dr. Carson bristled. It was one thing to feel guilty, another to be threatened.

"I owe you nothing," he told Dr. Cliff.

"That may be true." Dr. Cliff's voice was grim. "But you are going to have some explaining to do to this girl's sister. You said you were engaged to Laurel. She is going to wonder why you acted in such a way her twin sister was nearly killed."

The wind went out of Dr. Carson's sails completely. He had forgotten for a moment even the reason he was here in this ghastly country with these primitive people. Taking the offensive he shot back, "So you lied to me! You did know Willow O'Hara was here."

Dr. Cliff's voice was sharp. "I did not lie. Willow has never been known as O'Hara in Vista d'Oro." His voice was menacing. "And she'd better not be until she announces it herself."

Again Dr. Carson could feel the veiled threat behind the words. He was silent the rest of the way into town, and when he got to the missionary's place, crept into his room, and went to bed early. He couldn't face Peter Thompson, even for supper. He hoped Laurel would come the next day. He had to get away from here before he went stark, raving mad.

But Laurel did not come the next day, nor the next. Willow lay in the hospital with a broken ankle, too weak and tired to even ask questions. Finally, after another three days Dr. Carson announced he was going back to Phoenix. He wrote a long letter to Laurel, begging her to come home, and mailed it on the way through Flagstaff. Then when he did get to Phoenix he wrote another letter, sending it in care of General Delivery, Phoenix. All he could do now was sit back and wait. But still Laurel did not come, either to Phoenix or to Vista d'Oro.

After the first few days Willow began to improve and was moved to her own bedroom at Mrs. Molly's. She never mentioned the encounter on the mesa, yet Mrs. Molly could see the longing in her eyes each time the mail was brought from town. The clinic had a special arrangement where the mail was picked up every second or third day, but nothing came to show there was a Laurel O'Hara in the world.

Willow grew thin, listless. The day came when Mrs. Molly told Dr. Cliff, "You'd better talk with her. She's nothing but skin and bones. I don't know what that Dr. Carson said to her, but it couldn't be worse than her sitting there staring out the window."

That evening Dr. Cliff and Peter Thompson came to visit Willow. After chatting for a moment and examining her ankle, now in a cast, Dr. Cliff called Mrs. Molly into the bedroom.

"I want you to hear this, too," he said

quietly. In his own words he told of Many Tears's last words. He told of her heart breaking when she knew Cloudy Willow was dead, and how she stole Willow and raised her as her own. When he finished, he softly added, "I never knew Mike O'Hara, but I wish I could have. Evidently he loved your mother more than anything in life, Willow. He couldn't stand Vista d'Oro without her, so he went away, taking with him what he thought was all he had left of Cloudy Willow, your sister Laurel. If he had known of you he never would have gone. But he didn't know. Of that I am convinced." Truth rang in the finality of his words. Willow looked at him with swimming eyes, a light in her eyes neither Dr. Cliff nor Peter had seen before.

"Then they were married! My mother and father! They loved each other and were happy. They wanted me, looked forward and planned for me!"

Only then did the three who loved Willow so much know the great mistake that had preyed on her mind so long. With the news of Mike O'Hara she was free. She was someone.

"I think I'll sleep now," she told them and in a few moments was sound asleep. Dr. Cliff checked her pulse. It was steady.

Smiling, he led the way out, pausing in the living room to tell Mrs. Molly and Peter, "She will heal now. It wasn't her body I was worried about, but her spirit. Just like the small bird who falls. You can set its wing, but if there is no heart to fly, it will never soar again." He cleared his throat of huskiness. "Willow can soar now."

As he and Peter walked back to the mission Dr. Cliff asked, "Will you tell her of your love now, Peter?"

The young missionary was silent for a long time. When he spoke there was an unusual bitterness in his voice.

"How can I?" They walked on a few steps, then he said, "I am sure Willow cares. But she has never been anywhere except Vista d'Oro. If Laurel does come, Willow has the chance for a new life, in a new world. How can I tie her down to me when she has never known anything else? What right do I have to expect her to give up all that is her heritage as Dr. O'Hara's daughter? They have a proud blood line. She will be accepted simply because of her father. Can I ask her to turn her back on that, for me?"

There was a depth of agony in his voice. Dr. Cliff thought he had known Peter well, but never had he suspected the depths of the man now making his greatest struggle.

Without a word he extended his hand.

"God bless you," Peter said simply, and with a great squeeze, left his friend at the clinic door.

The next day Dr. Cliff brought the picture of Laurel that Dr. Carson had left on his desk to Willow. Unutterable joy filled her face.

"My sister," she almost crooned the words. "She is beautiful." She didn't realize how very lovely she herself was as she clutched the paper tightly. It wouldn't be long until Laurel would come, Willow firmly believed that. But how would she greet her?

In the days that followed Willow regained her strength. In spite of the heavy cast she managed to hobble around a little, helping Mrs. Molly. She developed quite a talent for cooking simple dishes and was able to relieve Mrs. Molly by having lunch and dinner ready when she came home. The clinic was terribly shorthanded without Willow. She had been a great help. Dr. Cliff and Mrs. Molly were kept busier than ever.

Peter Thompson spent a lot of time with Willow during those lonely days when she was recuperating. He often stayed for lunch or dinner, too, praising her skill as a homemaker, teasing her a little about it.

In spite of his determination not to speak to Willow of his feelings, Peter's honest gray eyes gave him away. They followed her every move. Willow wondered why he did not speak aloud. The shadow that had hung between them, although it had only been in her own mind, had been removed once she found out about her father. Yet another strange wall seemed to be growing between them. She couldn't understand it. She alternated between despair and hope, but then she would think of Laurel and her face would take on a radiance almost unearthly. She was counting the days until her sister came.

Mrs. Molly watched and said nothing, but she was worried. What if Laurel did not come? What if after she considered the story she decided to leave things as they were? It would crush Willow. The very life would go from her. The days passed. It was over two weeks since Dr. Carson had gone. She should have been here by now if she was coming. How many places were there to visit on her journey?

The same fears were tormenting Dr. Cliff. He too could see how bound up in her unknown twin Willow was growing. He remembered the girl in Flagstaff. She looked as though she were pretty much used to doing things her own way.

Peter was concerned with his own fight. More and more he wanted to confess his love for Willow, ask her to be his wife and to share his life of service at Vista d'Oro. But he would not back down on the course he had set. Not for nothing did he have stern Scottish ancestors. They gave him the courage to do what he felt was right. Time enough later for all that, after Laurel came.

And so everything at Vista d'Oro for those four comrades rested on one happening — Laurel's arrival.

Only Willow held no fear. She didn't try to reason when or why Laurel would come, she only knew she was coming. Much of her time was spent in plans for her sister.

"I hope she gets here before snow flies," she would mention one time. "The leaves are getting so pretty now, I know she will like them." Or, "Will Laurel like Peter?" she would whisper to herself. "Oh, she must!"

Then one night a bitter wind swept out of the north. It left a skiff of snow, heralding the approach of winter to Vista d'Oro. It was cold on the desert at night now. Even though the sun still shone brightly during the day, the nights were too cold to go out without a heavy jacket. When Willow saw the leaves dying and dropping from the trees she at last began to have doubts. At first she kept them to herself, then voiced them to Mrs. Molly.

"What if Laurel can't get here? If she waits much longer we could be snowed in. Dr. Cliff said she only had a white Mustang. We use the jeep or station wagon in winter. Do you think she'll have trouble?"

Hiding her own fears Mrs. Molly briskly told her, "She can always write. We'll see she gets here."

Willow brightened. "I never thought of that."

But as the nights continued to get colder she wondered. It was now late October, almost a month since Willow's accident. Why didn't Laurel come?

Willow began to lose her confidence. As the weather grew colder, so did her hope of Laurel coming. Again she became the despondent girl who had spent those days in bed after her fall. She grew thin and pale once more. At last she seemed to accept the truth. Her sister was not coming. She remembered all Dr. Carson had said about Laurel's life and how she, Willow, could never fit in. Maybe Laurel felt that way, too.

Even Peter could not cheer up the listless

girl. Mrs. Molly tried to tempt her appetite with small treats, but she was so busy she had little time for extra work. Willow no longer was interested in cooking and helping around the house.

"She's just dying of a broken heart," Mrs. Molly sobbed on Dr. Cliff's desk one day. "Why don't you send that Laurel a telegram and tell her about Willow?"

Dr. Cliff looked at her steadily. "I did that a week ago, followed by a letter." He held up a letter from his desk. "It was returned today marked address unknown."

Mrs. Molly didn't answer. There really wasn't any more she could say. Dr. Cliff had done everything he could to help, but to no avail. Even Dr. Carson had no knowledge of Laurel. A stack of unopened letters lay on the table addressed to her and a telephone call from him to Dr. Cliff disclosed he hadn't seen nor heard of her since the Grand Canyon incident.

Meanwhile Willow was sinking into apathy. The burning question in everyone's mind was — where was Laurel?

Chapter 9

Blissfully unaware of all the trouble her disappearance was causing, Laurel and Aunt Jane were having the time of their lives. The morning they left the South Rim was clear and bright. In a few hours they were traveling the same U.S. 89 that Grant Carson would take later that day. But what a difference! To them, the stark country had its own beauty, to be admired and enjoyed because it was so different. When they passed the faded sign pointing off the road to Vista d'Oro, Laurel longingly looked at the winding, hard-baked earth.

"Do you want to go there now?" Aunt Jane asked, but Laurel shook her head.

"No, it isn't time yet." She hesitated, then asked shyly, "Aunt Jane, do you believe that people know when it is the right time for certain things, the way I feel about going to Vista d'Oro?"

"Certainly." The frankness in Aunt Jane's practical voice swept away any lingering doubts Laurel might have had. "Nine times out of ten we know exactly what to do and when to do it if we would only listen to that inner voice that can direct us."

"Inner voice." Laurel thought that over. "I like that. I suppose it is what some call conscience?"

Aunt Jane snorted. "More like common sense is what it is, Laurel. We get so worried about pleasing everyone who tries to tell us what to do we ignore what we know is right."

Laurel smiled mistily. "Aunt Jane, I'm glad I have you. Everything seems to fall into place when you talk like that."

Aunt Jane was silent for a moment, then pointed out the window. "There's a perfect example. If you had come here with some of your other friends who ridiculed the barrenness and primitiveness of this country, in all probability you would either have agreed with them or else kept silent. But because I had told you what it would be like, and you came expecting to find its own kind of beauty, your attitude has been completely different."

Laurel had to agree. "Yes, and I wouldn't have missed it for anything!" It was late afternoon now and they had crossed the Colorado River at Marble Canyon. The Vermillion Cliffs lay stretched along the highway, brilliantly red in the sunlight. They had decided not to take the Page-Glen Canyon trip at present. Although it seemed hard to believe in this heat, Aunt Jane told her the North Rim of the Grand Canyon closed October 15. If they wanted to see it, they would have to go now since it was already well into September. The Glen Canyon trip would have to wait.

After leaving House Rock Laurel was thrilled by the sight of great shaggy beasts along the roadway.

"Are they, yes, they are buffalo!" she exclaimed.

Aunt Jane nodded. "Yes, this is the Buffalo Range." Laurel drove slowly, craning her neck to see. What a change from her life in Phoenix! Again that strange wild calling inside stirred her deeply. She felt free out here, alive and free!

It was nearly dark when they reached the tiny settlement of Jacob Lake, and the evening had turned cold.

"Over seventy-nine-hundred feet here," Aunt Jane said, reaching to the back seat for sweaters. "We'd better stay here tonight. I don't want you to miss what's ahead by going on now." This suited Laurel. She had fallen in love with the rustic place. Dozens of rude cabins stood near a trading post store. A tiny restaurant was there, and the cabins were equipped for housekeeping.

"Oh, Aunt Jane," she cried impulsively.

"Let's just stay here for a while! We can cook on the wood stove in the cabin; you said you knew how. And look at those places to wander!" She longingly held her arms out to the pine-scented forests surrounding the tiny hamlet carved in the middle of the great forest.

"We'd better stay on our way out," Aunt Jane told her. "This will be accessible long after the North Rim is closed."

Reluctantly Laurel let herself be persuaded, although to her way of thinking nothing ahead could compare with Jacob Lake.

There was ice in the pan of water outside their door when Laurel and Aunt Jane awoke the next morning. The first reaching fingers of winter had touched the land with frost. Aunt Jane built a great fire in the wood stove and Laurel dressed in her warmest clothing, although by afternoon she knew she would have to shed some of it in the sun. It wasn't quite seven o'clock when they left Jacob Lake, Aunt Jane driving this time.

"I don't want you to miss a thing," she told Laurel. Laurel was spellbound. If she had loved the South Rim, something in this North Rim country plunged deep in her heart to glow there and become part of her. For thirty miles they drove through the

Kaibab Plateau, mountain meadows rolling back from the road to great stands of timber. They didn't speak much — it was almost holy in the early-morning hush. Now and then Aunt Jane would point out something of interest. Once it was the rare Kaibab squirrel, a huge black fellow with white tail.

"This is the only place in the world they live," she told the enthralled girl.

A little later she said, "Look!" and to the left of the highway a flock of wild turkey fed on seeds from the pinyon pine. There were deer everywhere.

A feeling of satisfaction and contentment settled on Laurel like a mantle. She felt herself a new person, close to the land around her, filling up inside her reservoir of strength. Whatever happened at Vista d'Oro would not drain her of this experience, she knew that.

"I want to bring Willow here," she told Aunt Jane, who looked at her with pride. Aunt Jane had always loved Laurel but never so much as in these days when they could be together in the land of her mother. As long as she could remember Aunt Jane had also loved this land. It was a growing experience, almost like seeing it through new eyes, to bring Laurel fresh from city life to share this place.

They took every side road, Point Imperial, Cape Royal, every road that led to the edge of the canyon. Even inexperienced Laurel could see the evidences of a higher country. The vegetation was different, the season itself was so much more advanced. Brilliant scarlet vied with yellow in attracting the attention. Drifts of falling leaves squished as she scuffed through them in her sturdy shoes, and over it all, that blue, blue Arizona sky, unpolluted by factory wastes and grime.

"Heaven could never be more beautiful," Laurel whispered, unwilling to disturb the quiet landscape with loud talk. Aunt Jane only nodded. She was too full for words.

They had been afraid they couldn't find accommodations at the North Rim, but because of the lateness of the season they were able to get lodging. Grand Canyon Lodge was practically right on the canyon rim. Their room overlooked a magnificent view, and impulsively Laurel signed the register for the rest of the season.

"I could never get tired of this place," she said quietly. In the weeks that followed she was tireless. There wasn't a trail she didn't explore, a walk through the campgrounds that she didn't take, many of them over and over. There was a mile-long nature walk along the rim's edge, and as she had sat in her promontory spot at the South Rim, so she now haunted the trails. She ate in the lodge restaurant and café, amazed at her growing appetite. She dreamed the cold evenings away in front of the fireplace in her room and spent hours on the little private porch.

Aunt Jane was equally happy. While her hiking was more limited, she loved the atmosphere. The only sadness was that it would too soon be over.

At last the calendar pointed to October 14. Today had to be their last day. There were tears in Laurel's eyes as they packed the car in readiness to leave the next morning. The lodge staff were almost apologetic. They had grown to admire Laurel and peppery Aunt Jane during their long stay.

"Will you be back next year?" they asked eagerly.

Laurel only smiled. "Perhaps." She knew she would be back, but didn't know when. As they drove away, it was all she could do to refrain from bursting into tears.

Wise Aunt Jane, seeing her emotion, gently reminded, "Don't forget, Laurel. You wanted to go back to Jacob Lake."

Laurel's face brightened. In the long, lovely days at the canyon she had all but forgotten Jacob Lake and its effect on her. There was still time before winter to spend a little while there. Facing ahead, spirits lifted, she thoroughly enjoyed the drive from the North Rim back through the Kaibab Plateau. Most of the leaves had fallen now, yet there was beauty in the stark white birches and aspen etched against the dark, dark green of spruce and pine. She was glad to be alive, and Jacob Lake lay ahead.

If she lived to be a hundred she would never forget Jacob Lake, Laurel thought. Never had she lived in such a peaceful state. Time seemed of no importance as she and Aunt Jane settled down in the small housekeeping cabin. The pines sighed and whispered outside her window, lulling her to sleep at nights. The horseback rides, hiking, and never-ending icy cold mornings and warm afternoons blended together in one grand spectacle before cold weather struck. A week passed, then another.

There had been snow flurries a few times, and one night Aunt Jane said quietly, "You know, Laurel, if we don't want to get caught in a real storm, we will have to leave very soon." She had been talking with some of the people who lived at Jacob Lake and they knew the signs.

Laurel nodded, yet pleaded, "Just a few more days, Aunt Jane."

Shaking her head, Aunt Jane said, "Well, maybe one more day, but we must leave Sunday at the latest." Saturday night they shivered on their way back to the cabin from the little store. Everything was packed and in readiness. The next day they would go. Laurel reluctantly consented, knowing she would be leaving part of her heart behind, even as she had done at the South Rim and the North Rim.

In the middle of the night a low moaning awakened Aunt Jane.

"Laurel, Laurel, wake up!" She shook the girl. "You're having a bad dream."

Laurel sat up in bed, trying to recognize her surroundings. "Oh, Aunt Jane," she cried. "It was terrible. Something is wrong with Willow, I know it is! I dreamed she was reaching out to me, calling me. Aunt Jane, I've got to get to Willow!"

"There," soothed the good woman. "We'll leave tomorrow and go straight to Vista d'Oro. She's all right. What could be wrong?"

"I don't know," Laurel replied, shaking from the coldness of the cabin and from her dream. "I just feel she needs me. I could see her by a window, waiting for me! Oh, Aunt Jane, we must go as soon as daylight comes. It's about a hundred miles. We should be able to get there in a few hours, even over that road leading in from the main highway. Willow needs me, I can feel it."

Aunt Jane tucked her back in the warm blankets, promising, "All right, Laurel, we'll leave as soon as morning comes."

But when morning came, so did the first few flakes of snow. Lazily they drifted out of the leaden sky, lightly touching the hard, cold ground. Aunt Jane had insisted that Laurel eat something hot before they started and the trading-post people tried to talk them out of going.

"You'd better wait until tomorrow," an old-timer told them. "That's a nasty wind rising. If you get out on the road between Vermillion Cliffs and Echo Cliffs it can be mean. Better stay a little while longer. If we get snowed in, so what? You can go when it's cleared out. This is early for a storm, it won't last long. Better wait."

Laurel thanked him but would hear none of it. She confided to Aunt Jane, "We *have* to go. Willow is in some kind of trouble. We can't wait."

The storm was even worse than the

old-timer feared. By the time they reached Marble Canyon it was snowing hard. The highway was white in spots, although the rising wind had kept it fairly clean. The service-station attendant urged them to stay there and see if the storm would lift.

Laurel looked at the growing storm, then remembered her dream. Again she could see Willow reaching out, calling for her. Stubbornly she set her lips in a grim line.

"I have to go on," she said quietly. "Aunt Jane, if you like you can stay here, and I'll come back as soon as I can. But I have to go."

Aunt Jane felt a thrill shoot through her. How much her beloved country had taught Laurel! She replied, "There's no question of my staying, if you go, so do I."

The concerned service-station attendant shook his head at the "fool tourists" who wouldn't listen to his advice, but dug out an old pair of chains he said they could use. He showed Laurel how to put them on if she needed them on the road to Vista d'Oro. And with another mutter at her headstrong behavior, waved them good-bye.

The going was pretty easy until they came to the turnoff. Both Aunt Jane and Laurel had been searching intently so they wouldn't miss it. Once they were on it they felt better. It was only about twenty miles or so in — it couldn't get all that bad. But as the now-deepening snow began to pack in their wheels Laurel took the precaution to put on the chains. She realized they had almost waited too long.

"One good thing," she said brightly. "Even if they don't want us at Vista d'Oro, they'll be stuck with us! It looks as if this is going to last a while." A sob broke in the middle. In spite of all the weeks of peace, now that the time was almost here, the old fear rushed through her. What would she find at Vista d'Oro? Aunt Jane wanted to comfort her, but didn't know what to say. After all, neither of them had any way of knowing if or what Willow knew about Laurel and Dr. O'Hara. The only thing Laurel had to go on was her own instinct and the vivid dream of the night before. It planted a seed of hope in her heart, even as she slowed for a snow-covered rock in the road. All her concentration was needed for her driving. She mustn't worry about what she might find ahead. She had enough to worry about just getting there. The snow continued to fall, the wind began to make drifts.

Slower and slower went the Mustang

until on top of a slight rise Aunt Jane cried out, "There, Laurel, ahead! That light — it must be Vista d'Oro!"

Flexing her tense shoulder muscles, Laurel carefully kept the car in the path and at last stopped before the gate of a small house on the edge of town. With a prayer of thankfulness she told Aunt Jane, "I'll inquire here where the clinic is. I suppose that's where we should go first." Stepping out of the car she edged around the front, made her way to the porch, and raised her hand to knock.

That morning Mrs. Molly had taken Willow an especially attractive breakfast. It was Sunday and there were no overnight patients in the clinic, so she could take the time to fuss a bit. Willow greeted her with a warm smile. Her once beautiful face was thin and white. Mrs. Molly quickly bustled about to hide her emotion. Pulling the curtain aside she commented, "Look, Willow! It's snowing. Isn't it beautiful?"

Willow turned her head for a look out the window, then replied in such a soft tone that Mrs. Molly had to bend near to hear the words.

"She isn't coming."

The hopelessness of her voice brought

157

tears to Mrs. Molly's eyes.

"She can't come now, Willow. But this is an early storm. It won't last long. Then she can come." There was no need to name Laurel. Both knew of whom Willow was speaking.

Willow shook her head. "She's not coming at all, Mrs. Molly. I prayed to the Great Spirit and to Peter's God. If she was coming she would have been here by now." Pointing to the calendar with a slender hand, she said, "It's November first, far too late."

Her voice quivered and one tear quietly slipped to the sheet.

Mrs. Molly in her heart felt familiar anger rise for the unknown Laurel, but she only said, "Will you be all right for a little while, Willow? The children are singing a special song at Peter's service this morning and they asked me to come. I'll stay if you'd rather."

"No, go on." Willow attempted a feeble smile. "I'll just lie here and look at the snow."

After Mrs. Molly had gone, Willow pulled her heavy robe closer about her. She tried to remember how Mrs. Molly had said Laurel would still come to her, but the effort was too great. She was so tired. Maybe if she slept. . . . Resting her head back against the pillow, in a few moments she was sound asleep.

What was that harsh sound? Struggling up through the depths of sleep, she listened. There it was again, a strange knocking. Rousing herself, she wondered why Mrs. Molly didn't let the person in. Then she remembered. Mrs. Molly had gone to church. Well, she would just stay quiet. Everyone in the village knew she seldom got up now. They would realize Mrs. Molly was gone and come back later. She closed her eyes again, wishing the knocker would go away.

Again came the knocking. At last in desperation she knew she would have to go to the door herself. It was a long trip from the bed to the front door. Willow braced herself several times against various pieces of furniture, but finally she managed to get the door open. A gust of wind tore it from her, thrusting the stranger on the porch inside. Together they shut the door, then the stranger turned to throw back the hood covering her lustrous dark hair.

When Willow saw the face of the stranger she held out her arms, a strange animation highlighting her face.

"You came, oh, you came!" The joy in her

eyes lighted a spark in the matching blue eyes of the stranger. With a great cry she reached out for her sister. Laurel O'Hara had come home.

Chapter 10

Aunt Jane shivered as she opened the Mustang door and stepped out. Although it had only been a few minutes since Laurel disappeared into the house, the nippy air was doing its work well. She was glad she had on warm slacks and a heavy jacket. So this was Vista d'Oro! She looked around curiously. In all her Arizona experience she had never been in this particular place. A row of simple houses formed a roughly defined street. Further back there were a few hogans, reminiscent of pre-mission days. The low white building at the end of the street must be the clinic, and there was a small chapel across from it.

It was too cold to stand there looking around. The gently falling snow softened the starkness of this Indian village, covering it with a dignity of nature. Aunt Jane felt a strange peace steal over her. Would Laurel find welcome here in this quiet spot? She certainly hoped so. The weeks of vacation had deepened the color in Laurel's face as well as smoothed away the fatigue and sorrow from Dr. O'Hara's death.

"Aunt Jane!" Laurel was running down

the path, fear in her face. "Come quickly! It's Willow, she recognized me, then collapsed!" Together the young nurse and the motherly woman gently lifted Willow to the couch. Fumbling in her purse, Laurel drew out the smelling salts she always carried, and in a few moments Willow opened her beautiful eyes and smiled.

Aunt Jane was amazed. Except for the thinness of her face, the girl on the couch was an exact replica of Laurel. Even the same spirit seemed to glow far behind those wonderful blue eyes, filling her face with light.

"I'm all right," she murmured weakly. "I was so afraid you wouldn't come." She tried to go on but Laurel gently laid her hand over Willow's trembling lips.

"I'm here for as long as you want me," she said quietly, her eyes meeting Aunt Jane's in a long, level look. Aunt Jane nodded in agreement. The girl on the couch needed care, and Laurel was equipped to give it. Without asking, Aunt Jane quickly found the kitchen and heated some broth for Willow. It looked to her as though what the girl needed now was simply rest, food, and the will to live. Laurel had brought the last; Aunt Jane could help with the first two.

Carefully carrying it to Willow, Aunt Jane

gently fed her the broth, spoonful by spoonful. Laurel was delighted to see her eat it all.

When Willow had finished, they helped her back to her own room and she fell asleep almost immediately. Laurel and Aunt Jane quietly waited in the living room for Mrs. Molly to return from church. It seemed almost impossible that it was not yet quite noon. Even though they had left Jacob Lake very early, the snow gave the day such a gray look it felt later.

"How lucky Mrs. Molly left a light in the window," Laurel exclaimed.

Aunt Jane agreed, with a laugh. "It looked encouraging from the top of that murky hill!" She sobered and asked Laurel, "What do you plan to do? I believe Willow needs you."

Laurel slowly replied, "I know she does. I meant what I told her, I will stay as long as she wants me. But what about you, Aunt Jane? This is a rugged country. I don't want you to feel obligated to stay here unless you want to. You can always go on to Phoenix. We may not even be able to get accommodations here."

Aunt Jane laughed again. "Child, I'm used to roughing it! Give me a warm place with a roof over my head and I'll be happy

— as long as I'm with you."

Laurel gave her a look far deeper than gratitude. After a moment's silence she spoke. "I think maybe while Willow is sleeping I'll walk up to the clinic. I need to see the doctor, what was his name? Oh yes, Dr. Cliff Barclay. Since he knows about me, it seems right to contact him first. Anyway, if I'm going to stay here for a while, maybe I can volunteer my services in the clinic. I doubt that he has too much help!"

Aunt Jane looked at her as she rose and stretched. Laurel had never been more lovely than in the turquoise slacks and ski jacket she was wearing. Her dark hair gleamed against the white fur-like lining of the hood, and her eyes reflected the blue outfit.

"You look pretty glamorous for a nurse," she told the girl, but Laurel only laughed.

"The doctor will probably be so busy he will never notice. Besides, he's probably a woman hater or he wouldn't be out here." A sudden thought caught her breath. "Unless he's like Dad."

"He might be," Aunt Jane said. "Seems to me it takes a special kind of man to give up all the opportunities that doctors have to spend his life working in a small place like this."

164

"Well, I'll soon find out." Laurel zipped the jacket higher. "He may be in church, but I can leave a note and ask him to come here. I'm sure he has been taking care of Willow." A frown crossed her brow.

"I also have a few questions to ask Dr. Barclay. I want to know just what's wrong with my sister."

It didn't take long for Laurel to walk the short street from Mrs. Molly's house to the clinic. There was a light inside, and the door was unlocked so she stepped inside. To her surprise the waiting room, though small, was immaculate. Never had she seen such an attractive small room. There were Indian blankets, various pictures, and dried arrangements here and there, brightening the white walls with color. A tiny alcove had bright rugs on the floor and a few stuffed animals, obviously for the youngsters who came in. Laurel smiled at the worn teddy bear. Evidently it was a favorite. A few chairs made up the waiting area, but there was none of the chill usually found in doctors' waiting rooms.

Curiosity getting the best of her, Laurel slipped out of her jacket and peeked through the partly open door leading into what was evidently a small ward. Again she was amazed at its spotlessness. The snow outside was no whiter than the neatly folded sheets on the beds, again made cheery with Indian blanket coverings. The walls were a pale aqua, and although the room was empty there was a friendly feeling inside. She peeked into the little surgery and marvelled. How could this Dr. Cliff Barclay carry on his work in such a small space? Yet her respect grew. He must really be some doctor to take care of both the Vista d'Oro people and those from the huge radius that must come to the clinic.

Feeling a bit guilty, she hurried back to the waiting room when she heard footsteps outside the building. She barely made it when the door swung inward, followed by an Indian lady and a small child. The woman was pressing the little boy's hand tightly but blood was running through her fingers.

"Dr. Cliff!" she gasped, wildly looking around the room.

"He isn't here," Laurel admitted, her eyes never leaving the hand the little boy was doubling up in pain. "Bring him here."

The woman stared at her in surprise, hesitating for a moment, but Laurel seized the child, her fingers finding a pressure point with one hand, the other reaching to the desk behind her where she had noticed a great stack of clean, folded towels. Grabbing one, she pressed it to the deep cut, being careful not to frighten the child.

Knowing she couldn't work there at the desk, Laurel commanded, "Open the door," motioning to the ward. There was a fully equipped first-aid setup at the nurse's desk, she had noticed that earlier. At least she could bandage the cut tightly until Dr. Cliff was located.

The authority in her voice was enough for the woman, and she held the door while Laurel led the boy through, keeping her makeshift bandage in place with a firm hand.

The round-eyed little boy eyed her with suspicion as she lifted him to the desk top and reached for a pair of bandage scissors. With a scream of terror he jerked himself free, loosening the towel Laurel had wound around his hand.

Too late Laurel realized the scissors she had planned to use for cutting open the sterile pack of bandages had frightened him. It took three attempts, after putting the scissors back, to coax him from behind his mother, who was also looking at Laurel suspiciously but with growing recognition. In the tussle Laurel's carefully pinned-up hair had swung loose and her resemblance to

Willow was marked.

The woman made her decision. "Willow!" she pointed to Laurel, meanwhile pushing her son toward the young nurse. The boy's screams hesitated for a moment. In the confusion no one had heard the door open.

"Who are you and what are you doing in my clinic?" a gruff voice demanded. There was something familiar about his barking tone, but Laurel was too busy to even look up.

Continuing to hold the compress on the cut she snapped, "I'm Laurel O'Hara, a nurse, and I'm helping a hurt child!" There was sarcasm in her voice. The man should have been able to see what she was doing.

The gruff tone of his questions melted before the gentle fingers that replaced her own on the little boy's hand. "We'll have to take a few stitches," he told her. Quickly he directed her to the supplies, and in a short time the wound was cleansed, stitched, and bandaged. The little boy's tears dried in an amazingly short time at sight of the big apple the doctor produced from the small refrigerator in the store room.

It wasn't until everything was over and the patient and mother gone that Laurel had time to look up at the big man who now removed heavy coat, cap, and muffler. When she did, she couldn't believe her eyes.

"You!" The startled exclamation hung in the air. "Who are you?"

His voice was an exact imitation of her own as it had been earlier.

"I'm Clifford Barclay, and I am a doctor." His mocking voice brought a wave of red from hairline to chin.

"Dr. Cliff Barclay?" she echoed. Her mind whirled, then steadied. The man who had taken her father's place at Vista d'Oro, Dr. Cliff Barclay, was also the man who had so rudely grabbed her and stared so many weeks ago in the Flagstaff restaurant. To her horror, her irrepressible sense of humor bubbled over, leaving her laughing and helpless. The doctor looked at her icily.

"I fail to find anything humorous about my name," he told her curtly, turning away to discard the used materials from the accident. Laurel only laughed harder. She couldn't explain that first the shock of finding Willow, then the hurt child, and last of all, his unexpected identity had unbalanced her usually steady control.

Suddenly Dr. Barclay violently seized her and pressed his mouth to hers, hard, and held it there. Stunned, Laurel couldn't even move. An amused smile crossed his face.

"Can't have you getting hysterics," he smoothly explained. Fury filled Laurel. How dare he! What an insufferable man! She would sleep in the street before asking his help! Then she remembered. It wasn't for her, it was for Willow.

Bowing her head meekly so he couldn't see the mutiny in her eyes, she said sweetly, "Thank you so much. Of course you don't want hysterical nurses in your clinic. Believe it or not, I have never had hysterics in my life." The smile she gave him was a masterpiece, considering the rage in her heart.

He seemed taken aback, but only for a moment.

"I suppose you want to know about Willow," he stated flatly. "I can see no other reason you would be here."

Forgetting her anger, Laurel leaned forward, a tremble in her voice. "Is she all right? What exactly is wrong with her?"

Dr. Cliff's pent-up rage at the way Dr. Carson had caused Willow's accident spilled over and hoarsened his voice.

"Your fiance came up here and started the whole thing. If you had to send someone instead of coming to tell her yourself, why did you pick that —" He bit off the last word.

There was no acting as Laurel whitened.

"Grant? Here? What could he have to do with Willow?"

"Plenty. Thanks to him, she almost was killed falling off a ledge."

Laurel covered her face with her hands, then, raising her head, looked directly into Dr. Cliff's eyes. "I didn't know," she whispered. "I left no forwarding address. I wanted to think before I came to Willow. Your letter to my father hadn't said if she knew about me. I didn't know if I would be welcome." There was a forlorn sound in her words.

Dr. Cliff's manner thawed a bit. "You're very welcome, Miss O'Hara." He gestured to the telegram and letters on the desk, bypassing them to show her the returned letter he had sent to Phoenix. "I have been very worried about Willow. She was so excited, counting the days until she thought you would come. When the weather got stormy she started to lose hope. It has been all Mrs. Molly could do to even get her to eat." He went on to sketch the things Willow had told them, stressing her feeling of being no one, all of which had been changed by Many Tears's revelation concerning her father and, especially, Laurel.

"Thank you," Laurel said simply, extending both hands. She knew now why this strange, rugged man had been so antagonistic to her. It had been caused by worry over Willow. Anxiously she asked again, "About Willow?"

The doctor spread his hands out on the desk. Laurel noted the strength, yet remembered how gently he had worked with the injured child. At last he spoke.

"Technically there is nothing wrong with her. She has worried herself into a state of delicacy. I think your coming, if you plan to stay" — he glanced at her for her nod of assent — "will be the best medicine there is. However, winters at Vista d'Oro can sometimes be hard. I would like to see her in a warmer place for a while."

There was no hesitation in Laurel's response. "Like Phoenix?"

"Like Phoenix," he replied. "It could do her a world of good, not only the climate, but the chance to be in a different world for a time."

"Then she must go." Laurel was positive. "When will she be able to travel?"

In spite of his earlier feelings Dr. Cliff began to feel a spark of admiration for the decisive young woman before him. Ignoring the implications the visit might have in her own life, she hadn't paused a moment.

"I think she would be ready by

Thanksgiving," he said. "That gives her almost a month to recuperate. If you could keep her until spring, she would have a chance to build up all the strength that has been sapped by these last few weeks."

He hesitated slightly, then added, "Is there any reason you wouldn't want Willow in Phoenix?" He gestured to the pile of letters addressed to Laurel in Grant Carson's clearly visible writing.

"None whatsoever," Laurel responded composedly, heart beating fast. Something made her add, "He is not my fiance, by the way."

Why her statement should bring warmth to both faces was something neither had time to consider at that moment. It was enough for Laurel that this man before her, as dependable as the rocks from which he took his name, had spoken to her of Willow without trying to soften exactly what he meant. Impulsively she asked, "Dr. Barclay, I will be here that month. Could you use me in the clinic?"

"Could I!" Dr. Cliff's face shone as though heaven itself had opened up in front of him. Thrusting out his big hand, he said, "You're hired!"

A lump rose in Laurel's throat as she wordlessly took his hand. Again she could not explain why the approval of this stranger meant so much to her. Suddenly remembering, she said, "But where can Aunt Jane and I live?"

Dr. Cliff had already been thinking of that, and his reply was instantaneous. "I have a two-bedroom cottage behind the clinic. It was once your father's. You and your Aunt Jane can use it for your stay."

Laurel gazed at him misty-eyed. For him to know how much it would mean for her to stay there touched her deeply. "But where will you stay?"

Dr. Cliff smiled. "I can always bunk with Peter Thompson. He has an extra room." He failed to add, ironically, that the last person who had used the room had been Dr. Carson.

"What time do I report for duty?" Laurel asked, all business now that housing was settled.

"Tomorrow morning at seven. Take the rest of the afternoon to meet Mrs. Molly and be with Willow. Our hours are more or less on an 'on-call' basis, but we do get here early and set things up for the day. By the way" — he looked a bit shamefaced — "that will give me a little time to see what I can do about cleaning out my place. Bachelor quarters, especially doctors', tend to get pretty messy."

Laurel laughed outright. "Don't worry about that! Aunt Jane is never happier than when she has a house to clean. In a week she'll have the place so spotless you won't feel at home when you get back in it!"

Something flashed between them as Dr. Cliff held her ski jacket for her. "Then I'll see you tomorrow."

"Tomorrow," she promised. It wasn't until she had gone that Dr. Cliff noticed she had forgotten the pile of letters still on his desk in Dr. Carson's handwriting. A broad grin crossed his face as he swept them into a pile. For some reason he felt extremely light-hearted, and for the first time since Willow's accident he whistled on his way to his cottage, determined to spend a little time cleaning, Aunt Jane or no Aunt Jane!

The rest of the day flew. Laurel and Aunt Jane loved Mrs. Molly on sight, and she insisted on helping them get settled.

"No trouble at all." She beamed. "We're just so glad to have you here!" Peter Thompson was also invaluable. Glad to have this friend with him, even on a temporary basis, he moved Dr. Cliff's trappings to his own home while the women were invading the doctor's cottage. If an unusual ache in his heart persisted at the thought of

Willow going away soon, he covered it well. He had fought it out with himself and knew it must be.

As for Aunt Jane, she was in her element. There was nothing she liked better than cooking and cleaning. "None of this Women's Lib for me." She laughed. "My place is in the home taking care of others so they can be out working!" By night she and Mrs. Molly were fast friends and in addition to helping care for Willow, Aunt Jane had volunteered to do any necessary cooking for overnight patients at the clinic and relieve Mrs. Molly in that area.

"Bless her!" Dr. Cliff exclaimed when Mrs. Molly tapped on his door and asked him to eat supper with them. He had liked Aunt Jane at first sight, and now he didn't know how to thank her except to assure her quietly how very much she would be appreciated.

Willow's quiet happiness filled the room. She had been allowed to get up for supper. "We don't call it dinner here," Mrs. Molly explained. "Dinner is the midday meal." For the first time Willow really did more than pick at the meal before her. Maybe it was the joy of those around the table, but her face sparkled with happiness. She couldn't take her eyes off Laurel across the table, so like her, yet with an inexplicable difference. In turn, Laurel was fascinated by this new sister. Peter Thompson watched them both, noting the quick intimacy that had already begun to grow between the long-separated twins. He had joined the party simply by announcing that since he had helped move he was staying for supper.

He had been pleased when at the beginning of the meal Mrs. Molly had told him, "Peter, we have much to be thankful for. I want you to ask a blessing on our food." His heartfelt prayer was echoed by each one present.

When Laurel tucked Willow into bed before leaving for her "new temporary home" she lovingly put her arms around her sister and held her close. Then, opening her purse, she read the words Dr. O'Hara had written just before he died. Willow's eyes were bright with unshed tears at the love story of their parents, but when Laurel read the closing words of her unknown father — "I hope someday you will find her . . . And if you do, tell her I didn't know . . . and ask her to forgive" — she grasped Laurel's hand tightly. There was no need of words for her to express her feelings. They shone in her face.

Laurel was surprised when she stepped

outside and found Dr. Cliff waiting.

"I thought you might want company," he said rather awkwardly. "Mrs. Molly and Aunt Jane have already gone over to the house. It is a strange town, different from what you're used to." His voice seemed to gain assurance as he walked with he r the short distance. He told her of the very little crime in the village, usually caused by outsiders. It was perfectly safe for the girls to roam free as long as they were in sight of Vista d'Oro. There had never been any trouble with anyone being followed or harmed in any way.

"That's why Willow was so frightened up on the big mesa," he added grimly.

Laurel started to say something, but stopped. Now was not the time to disclose the entire story of Dr. Carson.

Seeming to read her mind, Dr. Cliff asked, "Do you want to go by the clinic and get your letters?"

He hadn't realized he had been holding his breath until Laurel answered crisply, "I wish you'd burn them. I do not care to read anything from Dr. Carson, either now or later."

There was something in her voice that prohibited Dr. Cliff from asking anything else, but again his heart leaped inside in a very strange way. Don't be foolish, he told himself, she's not for you. Yet when he bid her good night at the door to his house there was a gladness that didn't escape Laurel's notice as he said, "I'm glad you've come, Laurel. It will mean a great deal." He stopped, then started to add something else, but instead merely said good night and strode off in the darkness.

Laurel stood staring after him curiously. I wonder what he meant by that, she thought, it will mean a great deal to whom? "To Willow, of course," she muttered under her breath sternly, but there was color in her face when she opened the door that had not been put there by the crisp night air.

Chapter 11

The time between Laurel's arrival in Vista d'Oro and her departure flew by on golden wings. Strangely enough, never in her life had she been so contented. Her work with Dr. Cliff at the clinic was all-satisfying. Even though she had always been a conscientious worker, back in Phoenix there had been many others to take her place when she wasn't there. Here there were no substitutes. She marvelled how the doctor with only Mrs. Molly and Willow's help had accomplished what he had done, and deep inside a tiny spark was lighted. What was to prevent her coming back after Willow's winter in Phoenix? Putting the thought aside to be thoroughly digested later, she plunged wholeheartedly into her work.

Laurel was learning to love the courteous dark-skinned people who came to their clinic. She never knew how Dr. Cliff explained her presence to them, she only knew their shy smiles were welcoming. When she walked down the street or into the tiny store, there was always someone with a friendly greeting. Contrary to her preconceived ideas, all but a very few of the older villagers spoke English quite well. She in turn was beginning to catch on to a few of the Navajo words, loving the liquid sound of the soft language.

Willow was improving steadily. All she had needed was something to live for, as Aunt Jane had thought the very first day they arrived. Sometimes alone she wondered how she could be so fortunate. She was excited about going to Phoenix with Laurel and Aunt Jane, yet a natural timidity caused her to ask over and over, "Will I be afraid? Will the people there like me?"

Aunt Jane laughed at her fears, her fond gaze resting on the anxious face. "As pretty as you are, you'll need a stick to keep the young men away from our door." She rolled her eyes in mock despair. "How I will ever get anything done with two such beautiful girls in my care certainly is beyond me!"

Willow blushed. During her growing-up years she had never thought of herself as pretty, but seeing Laurel and knowing she was a reflection had given her a great deal of self-confidence. Besides, if Laurel and Aunt Jane thought she was pretty, she must be. Her faith in them both was implicit.

Dr. Cliff had found Laurel as competent as any nurse he had ever known. She seemed to anticipate his every need, and the patients loved her. More and more he came to rely on her, dreading the day she would leave. He firmly disciplined the thoughts that strayed to her loveliness as well as her efficiency. He had known when he chose the life in Vista d'Oro there was little probability of the kind of woman he would choose being willing to spend her life in the desert. Yet at times he caught a look in her eyes that thrilled him to the very soul, a sharing of interests, or appreciation of some little moment.

To make up for the early snowstorm, the weather had changed to a beautiful November. Crisp, cold nights. Afternoons sunny enough to lay warmth over the land. Color everywhere, in the leaves, the mesas, even the very soil itself. A few days before they were to leave, Willow directed Laurel to the path leading to the big mesa. She confided how over the years it had been her refuge, and when Dr. O'Hara's story had been told, she knew why. It had also been his. Although she wasn't yet physically strong enough to climb the trail, she wanted Laurel to see it, so late one afternoon Laurel took the path upward until she stood for the first time above the little village.

The same peace and quietness that had drawn first her father, then her twin, now rested on Laurel. Many weeks ago she had awakened far away knowing that moment was one of sheer happiness, to be remembered. So it was this day. The same great pinyon provided cover, the same mellowing of the day lay its golden patina over the view below her.

I could be happy here the rest of my life, she thought, and the truth struck her. These were her people, even as her father had known they were his. She would take Willow to Phoenix, but in the spring, she would bring her back. Then if Dr. Cliff wanted her, she would stay. How long she did not know. It seemed unnecessary even to plan at this time.

Slowly she made her way home to the village in the last rays of sunlight and before the evening chill could set in. The time on the mesa had given her a look of determination, and it was with a happy face she greeted Willow at the door, noting how rounded her cheeks were growing as she regained her health. In fact, it was becoming more difficult daily to tell the girls apart. Some of the children in the village called them both Willow or Laurel, depending on which name they thought of first! It amused both girls, and Laurel promised Willow when they reached Phoenix they would go shopping for new clothes. Although she didn't need them herself, she wanted Willow to be able to choose what she liked. Perhaps they would even buy one outfit alike and see how much fun they could have fooling the Phoenix crowd.

Laurel often thought of her first reaction to Dr. O'Hara's letter. She would never confess to this sister how at one time she had even considered destroying the letter or bribing Dr. Cliff. The last thought brought a laugh. Never in any way could she imagine Dr. Cliff taking a bribe, for any reason! His eyes would flash fire at the very mention of such a thing. In the weeks she had worked with him only once had his temper flared, and that was for just cause. A child had died because the parents had not followed his advice with the proper medication. Laurel would never forget his stony look of suffering. She treasured the glimpses she had seen of the warm-hearted man inside the cool professional exterior. Somehow she felt those were times when the real Dr. Cliff showed.

On Thanksgiving morning Peter held a special service in the little chapel. There were no patients in the clinic at that time so all were free to attend. For the first time Willow was allowed to go, and her joy was

184

evident in the way she greeted those who spoke to her.

Laurel and Aunt Jane felt the same sense of worship that had been in the little white church in Globe the first day of their trip. Peter spoke simply, stressing the joy those first settlers knew as the crops were harvested after the hard year. He told how without Squanto's help they would all have starved, and closed with a simple prayer. The children had learned a song of thankfulness. First they sang it in English, then in Navajo. Laurel was touched by the blending of the two cultures in this little village, and especially there in the chapel.

It had been decided that Laurel, Willow, and Aunt Jane would get an early start the next morning. Phoenix was quite a drive.

Thanksgiving evening, when Laurel looked from her window, she could see there was still a light in the clinic. That's strange, she thought, we had no patients today. Calling to Aunt Jane that she would be back in a minute, she caught up her heavy jacket and quickly walked to the lighted building. Everything was quiet and still in the waiting room. A lump rose to her throat as she remembered the happy hours of service she had given there. Dropping into a comfortable chair, she let her feelings give way.

Laurel didn't know how long she cried, but suddenly she was aware that she was no longer alone. Hastily brushing away the tears, she looked up to see Dr. Cliff in the doorway to the ward, a tender look on his face.

"Who are you and what are you doing in my clinic?" His gruff tone was belied by the twinkle in the blue eyes.

Laurel laughed through her tears. "I'm Laurel O'Hara, a nurse, and I don't want to leave." A fresh flood filled her eyes.

With a giant stride the doctor was beside her, gathering her into his arms. "Oh, Laurel!" She clung to him, sobbing as though her heart would break. For a long time he held her close, not saying anything, then held her off from him.

"I'm not good at fancy speeches. I wasn't even going to say anything to you before you left, but Laurel, I love you. I can't let you go back to Phoenix without telling you how I feel."

A skyrocket seemed to burst in Laurel's heart, and a radiance filled her face that gave her an unearthly beauty.

"Oh, Dr. Cliff," was all she could say. It was enough. The doctor had his answer. Gently he drew her to him again in a long kiss.

When they recovered a bit, Dr. Cliff talked to her seriously. "You know what a hard life it is here. It's all I can offer you, Laurel. My place is here with my people." He hesitated, then continued.

"You come from a different world. That world has now stretched to include Willow. Your heritage as Dr. O'Hara's daughter is among a different class of mankind. Are you sure you can give it up without regret? I know you have learned to love Vista d'Oro, but you've only spent a month here. It is a short time compared to the years that will lie ahead if you marry me. You have to be sure that's what you want."

There was no hesitation on Laurel's part. "It's what I want," she said quietly. She couldn't put into words what Vista d'Oro had given her, but her eyes spoke for her. Convinced at last, Dr. Cliff smiled.

"Then there will be a wedding in the spring."

Laurel's heart fell. "We have to wait that long? Why can't I send Aunt Jane and Willow to Phoenix and stay here for the winter? I know Mrs. Molly would put me up if you don't want to marry me that fast!" There was mischief in her voice.

Dr. Cliff's heart leaped, but he sternly put the temptation aside.

187

"No, Laurel, I want you to go back among your own people until spring. This will give you time to think things over. If you decide it is too much to give up, I will understand. When you are among your own people you may feel differently."

"I am among my own people now," she told him.

For a moment he almost weakened, but then he insisted. "Willow will need you. It's a new world for her, too. I know Aunt Jane loves her but she needs you. It won't be long until spring."

Again she clung to him, but at last he gently set her aside. "It's getting late and you have an early start." There was a little doubt in his voice as he said, "Are you going to tell Willow and Aunt Jane?"

Laurel considered for a moment. "I'll tell Aunt Jane but not Willow. If she knew she might not go." Dr. Cliff nodded in agreement. Willow was proud. It might be best to keep it a secret for now.

Laurel kissed him good night. "Don't come with me. I need a few moments to get collected before going in." From the window he saw her start toward the house, then on impulse turn toward the chapel across the street. To think that such a wonderful girl loved him! It was almost beyond his wildest dreams! He chuckled a bit. Now if only Peter and Willow . . . The thought accompanied him as he closed the clinic door and went back to the nurse's desk to check a few charts before retiring.

Across the street Laurel paused, then slipped inside the chapel. A ray of light from some hidden source vaguely illuminated the small room. Peter had told her the Navajos didn't like darkness in the chapel — they thought of it as a place of light — so he had installed the light to be on during all dark hours. It was always unlocked, and anyone who cared to could come and go freely.

She sat in the silence, drinking up the peace, her heart beating joyously. Gone was all memory of Dr. Grant Carson, who she had once thought she loved. He had been forever replaced by a tall, craggy doctor with burning blue eyes and sandy hair. A shiver of delight filled her as she thought of spring. Perhaps they could be married right here in the little chapel. She knew it would please him, and outside of Aunt Jane and Willow she really had no one she cared about seeing her married. Oh, there were friends in Phoenix, but they were casual. The ones who loved her would understand, and she didn't care what the others thought. Her home would be in Vista d'Oro, as her father had planned for his life to be, even in the same house.

The chapel was cold and Laurel began to shiver. Time to go. With a backward look she carefully closed the door behind her and stepped to the yard outside. Without warning she was seized from behind and a pair of strong arms held her close. Turning, struggling furiously, she looked full into the face of Peter Thompson!

"Laurel!" He was aghast. "I'm sorry . . . I thought you were Willow!" A light began to dawn in Laurel's brain.

"So that's how it is!" She grasped his hand warmly. "Oh, Peter, I am so glad!"

Peter shook his head somberly. "No, Laurel. That isn't how it is. I love Willow with all my heart and soul — but I don't know if she cares. Even if she does I have no right to speak."

"But why?" Laurel gasped. "Why not?"

Peter looked at her intently. "Willow has just discovered who she is. She needs to see something of the world besides Vista d'Oro. As long as she was Navajo, at least in everyone's eyes, things were different. Now she must see and experience the white world." His voice was desolate.

Compassion filled Laurel. She sensed greatness in this simple missionary. He was making a fight, not for himself, but for Willow.

"I think if I said one word asking her to stay she would," Peter said. "But I can't do it. I'm glad it was you instead of her. For a moment the thought of her going was too much. When I saw you, thinking it was Willow, I couldn't hold back. But it's best this way. She will go, and in time I suppose my work will dull the pain."

"But she will be back," Laurel cried. "Peter, I have seen her eyes follow you. All the cities in the world won't be able to hold her back. I think the only reason she is going is because you and Dr. Cliff insisted. She will come back!"

The conviction in Laurel's voice did what no amount of self-examination could have done for Peter. Hope burned within him, yet he had to ask, "How are you so sure?"

Taking a deep breath and feeling the warmth steal to her cheeks Laurel replied, "Because I am."

"You're coming back?" Peter was astounded. "You mean to bring her home?"

"Not exactly, you see." She paused and grew rosier. "I'm going to marry Dr. Cliff."

Peter was thunderstruck. He had sensed how Dr. Cliff had learned to depend on

Laurel but hadn't dreamed there was anything between them.

"How . . . when . . ." he stammered.

Laurel's clear laugh rang out in the night
air. "Just tonight." She sobered. "We aren't
saying anything to Willow. She needs these
months in Phoenix."

"Well, that's great!" Peter told her
heartily. "Do you mind if I congratulate
you?" Taking her consent for granted he
gave her a brotherly hug and kissed her
flushed cheek. "Now you'd better get home
before you catch cold."

"You sound like Dr. Cliff," she mocked,
but with another laugh ran up the street to
the clinic cottage. After a moment Peter,
still half dazed, stepped back into the clinic
and all was still.

Behind a window curtain, Willow, face
pale as death, sank back on her bed. When
she had heard Laurel's happy laugh she
peered through the glass. Just the sound of
her sister's laughter still brought happiness
to Willow. Frozen to the spot, she had seen
Laurel and Peter by the chapel door, and
the kiss that followed. At first she couldn't
believe it, yet as she lay awake during the
long dark hours of the night it all fell into
place. Of course they loved each other. How
could they help it? Peter, so dependable, so

different than that Dr. Carson who had wanted Laurel. Laurel, herself, bubbling, joyous — any man would love her.

Carefully she packed her own dreams away. Laurel must never know how she herself had felt. Nor must Peter. It wouldn't be too hard. She would be going away in the morning, perhaps without even seeing him. In Phoenix Laurel would have her work. She could keep her broken hopes well hidden, Willow decided. Then another thought struck her. Would Laurel be coming back to Vista d'Oro, or would Peter give up his mission work?

I will go wherever they won't be, she thought. If they return to Vista d'Oro I will find work in Phoenix, maybe take nurse's training. Laurel said Father's money was for my use too. I can stay with Aunt Jane. Or if they decide to live away from Vista d'Oro I can come home. I can go back to being "just Willow" and all the other will in time fade and be part of a dream.

Her decision firmly made, Willow at last closed heavy eyes and fell into a troubled sleep. But the pillow under the sleek black cloud of hair was wet with tears and a droop of sadness touched the beautiful mouth.

Chapter 12

Friday morning dawned bright and clear. It would be a beautiful day for the trip to Phoenix. Laurel looked anxiously at Willow. There were dark circles beneath her eyes and she looked as though she hadn't slept well.

"Are you all right?" she questioned, but Willow only nodded her head.

"I'm just tired." Two bright spots appeared on her cheeks and Laurel realized she was being torn two ways at the moment. Wisely she said no more, but busily helped Aunt Jane prepare a little nest for Willow in the back seat of the Mustang.

"This car isn't all that comfortable for three," she observed, laughing. "But we'll fix you up so if you get tired you can take a nap." Willow smiled wanly, knowing she wouldn't be able to sleep. She both anticipated and feared saying farewell to Peter and kept an eye on the door. Mrs. Molly had gone to the clinic earlier and now she rushed in, waving a note.

"Laurel, this is from Dr. Cliff." Laurel opened it curiously. Strange the doctor would send her a note just as he was due to say good-bye. Opening it she read:

Sorry Peter and I won't be there to say good-bye. Very early this morning a rider came in from the east and awakened us. One of the old women is sick and wants us both to come. I love you.

Cliff

"Dr. Cliff and Peter won't be able to come and tell us good-bye," she told the others. "They were called out this morning." She caught the strange look on Willow's face, a mixture of disappointment and relief. Laurel thought she understood. It would have been hard for Willow to keep from showing she cared in those parting moments. Secretly smiling to herself, she tucked the note in her purse. It wouldn't be all that long before Willow knew how much Peter cared. In the meantime, it was a long way to Phoenix.

At last they were in the car and on their way. Their last sight of Vista d'Oro was of Mrs. Molly standing in her doorway waving at them, then a bend of the road took them out of sight. Each of the three was occupied with various thoughts. Laurel longed to turn the little Mustang around and go right back to Dr. Cliff. Willow closed her eyes and let the pain of departure sweep over her, knowing the others would think she had fallen asleep. For her it was more than just leaving her home for a new world. She might not be coming back. Aunt Jane knew how much she would miss Vista d'Oro. Would she ever see it again? Laurel hadn't had time to confide in her or her fears would have been groundless. The good woman had seen Dr. Cliff's growing attachment for Laurel long before he spoke, but she had no way of knowing that things were settled. She only knew that she had been totally happy this last month. She and Mrs. Molly were bosom companions. Even if Laurel doesn't come back, Aunt Jane decided, I will. I'll come back whenever I can and stay with Mrs. Molly.

"You know, we're really very lucky," Aunt Jane reminded Laurel. "It could have been terrible weather for our trip."

Laurel nodded, keeping her eyes on the road. "Yes. Everything is turning out better than I dared hope." There was a lilt in her voice that caused Aunt Jane to look at her sharply.

"You certainly seem happy enough. I thought you would hate to leave Vista d'Oro, even with Willow coming along."

"I do," Laurel replied softly, not wanting to waken Willow. "But the sooner we go, the sooner we can come back." Her face turned red and Aunt Jane chuckled.

"I see. When did he tell you?"

Laurel wasn't even surprised that Aunt Jane had guessed her secret.

"Last night," she replied. "You know when I went out for a little while? It happened then. He wasn't going to say anything for fear I was too much of a city girl to want to live in Vista d'Oro. Then all at once he just had to speak, and I'm glad he did!"

Neither of them knew the pain being inflicted on Willow. Even though she had thought she had accepted the truth, yet hearing it in Laurel's own words thrust a new stab to her heart. If Laurel had only known what Willow was thinking! But she had no way of realizing what she was doing to her beloved sister as in low tones she went on to tell Aunt Jane her plans.

"He doesn't know it yet, but I'm going to sell the home in Phoenix unless you and Willow want it. He thought when I got back to town I might change my mind about him, but I know I won't. He's the most wonderful man in the world, giving his life for the people of Vista d'Oro! I can support him in his work, not financially for I know he would never consider it, but just by being there."

She paused, then went on. "Aunt Jane, I feel really alive to the important things of life. I know these next months will go swiftly, and then next spring I begin a totally new life. But what about you? And Willow? Suppose she likes Phoenix so well she wants to stay. What then?"

Aunt Jane smiled. "I don't think she will, Laurel. But if she does, I will be glad to stay with her as long as she needs me. She's part of you, you know." Again she smiled. "I rather think when spring comes Willow will be just as anxious to go home to Vista d'Oro as you are. If so, then that will be my home too."

Laurel gently took her hand from the wheel and laid it over Aunt Jane's. She was too choked up for words. What a perfect future lay ahead! Aunt Jane, Willow, and then Cliff! How could one person be so blessed?

"I wish we had time to go back to the Grand Canyon and Oak Creek Canyon," Laurel remarked when they arrived at Flagstaff. "I don't think we should, though. Willow looked terribly tired this morning, and it would make the trip a lot longer. But there will be long weekends this winter. If it stays open we may get back up for a visit. I can hardly wait to show Willow some of those wonderful places we visited! She will love them as much as we did. Aunt Jane, think of all the years we didn't have each other! Twin sisters, only a few hundred miles apart, yet not knowing of one another's existence. What if Many Tears had kept her secret?" A sob rose to her throat. "I don't see how I could ever have lived without Willow! It seems I should have felt that another part of me was somewhere."

Aunt Jane was silent for a long time. "Perhaps that's why you do love her so much, Laurel, because you never had the opportunity to grow together."

"We'll make up for it now," Laurel vowed. "I want Willow to see everything Phoenix has to offer. Of course, none of it is so wonderful as Vista d'Oro, but still I think she will enjoy the shops and restaurants. And won't she make a sensation among my friends! I can hardly wait!"

Slow tears seeped under Willow's lashes and she furtively wiped them away. In spite of the great loss in her heart, she was thrilled by the deep love Laurel held for her. She determined to never do anything to reflect on Laurel and to always make her happy. Even if it meant giving up Peter, she would do it. A little later she made a great fuss about stirring, then sitting up.

"Where are we? Did I miss all the scenery?" She eagerly looked out the window, her eagerness only half pretense. She had never been further south than Flagstaff and the country was very different. Small trees dotted the rolling hills. In the distance she could see larger bluffs that Aunt Jane said led to Zane Grey's cabin. Laurel remembered her feelings that day on the Mogollon Rim above the Tonto Basin where Zane Grey wrote and had to tell Willow all about it. "That's another place for us to go." She laughed.

Wistfully Willow returned the laugh, while inside she wondered how she could ever tell Laurel their paths wouldn't always be together.

It was getting dark when they reached Phoenix. No need for Willow to pretend sleep now. She was fascinated by the largeness of the city with its many colored lights. Aunt Jane told her the Christmas decorations were up, and they would go downtown to see them as soon as she was stronger. In spite of her unhappiness, Willow anticipated the many things she would see and learn.

When they drove into the yard of the O'Hara home, the house was ablaze with light. Aunt Jane had taken the precaution to make some calls and the Neilsons next door had gladly done the rest. Electricity and telephone service had been restored and Mrs. Neilson had even stocked the refrigerator and baked a fresh pie. Willow stared in amazement at the size of the home. She was almost frightened. Never had she been in a house so grand. The rich red carpet that sank under her feet; the charming lavender bedroom with adjoining bath that she would have, the roomy kitchen were all a little strange to her. What need did they have of such a large place? She wanted to know. She contrasted it with the small homes of Vista d'Oro, and her eyes sparkled. It would make her well just to live in this beautiful house of her father!

There was a large picture of Dr. O'Hara over the mantel, and when they returned to the living room and Laurel lighted a fire the flames flickered on his red hair and intense blue eyes. So this was her father. She stood for a long time gazing into the picture while Laurel waited breathlessly. At last Willow turned.

"His face is good." She said no more but both Laurel and Aunt Jane realized they had been holding their breath for Willow's approval, which she had expressed so simply. Among the Navajos a good face was very important. Not necessarily beautiful, just good. Dr. O'Hara had passed the supreme test.

It was odd how quickly Willow settled into the Phoenix home. She felt it reached out welcome arms to her from that unknown father who would have loved her if he had only known. While Laurel spent a few days getting ready to return to her old job for a few months, Willow spent hours in the sunlit yard or the little park. It was hard for her to understand how November and then December could be so warm. The friends Laurel introduced her to welcomed her warmly, for Laurel had chosen well. Dr. Carson was not one of them.

The first night they had arrived somehow Debi Thorne got wind of it. She made a beeline to the phone and called Grant.

"I see Laurel's back." Her tone was malicious.

"I knew she would be," he answered coolly, unwilling to admit he had known no such thing. Debi hung up, frustrated, yet planning to somehow gain his attention for herself. She needn't have bothered. When Dr. Carson arrived that evening after Willow had gone to bed, Laurel told him she had brought Willow home.

He drew himself up haughtily. "Then I must ask you to forget my offer of marriage," he told her coldly, and stalked out before she had time to tell him of her own engagement. Burning with fury, he spent a sleepless night, and the very next evening called Debi Thorne and invited her to dinner.

The glamorous redhead accepted with pleasure and Dr. Carson took her to the most expensive restaurant in Phoenix, one where all his friends would be sure to see them. Between dinner and the entertainment he drew the diamond that he had originally bought for Laurel from his pocket. He had decided the best thing to do was get engaged to Debi before Phoenix and more particularly Desert General discovered who Willow was.

Debi's eyes lighted at the size of the stone. There was something a little pathetic in the eager way she accepted it, and before the evening was gone several friends stopping by their table heard the news. It was in the following morning's papers, announcing an immediate wedding.

Debi had felt a moment's pang when she asked if Grant had seen Laurel and he blazed at her, "I don't care if I ever see her again!"

The girl was silenced but only smiled to herself. She knew how to keep a man interested, and now that they were engaged Dr.

Carson's playboy days were over. She was a curious combination of modern and old-fashioned in that once she had gotten her man she intended to hang on to him. By the end of the evening Dr. Carson had pretty much convinced himself he had never cared for Laurel and he was a lucky man to be marrying Debi, with her large green eyes.

Laurel laughed when she saw the picture in the paper. A few weeks later when the wedding invitation came she selected a choice gift and sent it with warm regards to them both. That chapter of her life was finished, and the high-society wedding pictures that followed didn't even cause a pang.

Willow gained rapidly but somehow she still had a shadow in her eyes. Aunt Jane wondered if she were homesick, but Willow shook her head. No, she wanted to be with Laurel. She spent hours with Aunt Jane while Laurel was working, learning all kinds of fancy cooking. On Laurel's days off they went shopping, and to Willow it was fairyland. Never had she seen such stores! Her taste was simple and in perfect taste for her own style. She hesitated a few times between garments, then chose what she thought Laurel would like. She had learned to appreciate Laurel's style and knew she wouldn't go far wrong in following suit.

If it hadn't been for Peter Thompson Willow would have been completely happy. But sometimes in the dark night hours when she couldn't sleep she lay listening to the traffic go by, thinking of Vista d'Oro — and Peter. Christmas Eve was a hard time for her. Laurel had asked if she would like to go out for dinner, but she preferred to stay home. Although she loved the big restaurants and their choices of new foods, most of all she loved the quiet evenings the three of them spent together. So that afternoon Aunt Jane stuffed squabs, made pies, cranberry sauce, and all the good Christmas things, and they stayed home for the evening.

A special telecast was being shown of the true Christmas story and as Willow watched it she thought of Vista d'Oro. Last year Peter had held a special Christmas Eve service. Everyone in the village had bundled up in their warmest clothing and huddled together in the little chapel. He had given the Christmas story and they had sung carols. Now as Willow watched the television it all rushed over her, leaving her more forlorn than she had been for a long time.

When the program ended there were tears

in Laurel's eyes. The story had been portrayed very movingly. Switching off the lights and curling up on the couch next to Willow, she said softly, "I wonder why television programs sometimes make us cry. They're just programs."

Willow was still for a moment then she replied, "It is because of the tears below the surface." Laurel didn't understand. Often Willow shared thoughts with her beyond her own knowledge.

Now she asked, "What do you mean, Willow?"

Willow chose her words carefully. "When you are young many times you stumble and fall, hurting yourself. You run crying to someone for comfort. But when you grow up, the world says you must not cry, it is a sign of childishness. So just beneath the surface are many tears, like our grandmother was named." She lapsed into silence but Laurel took up the idea.

"Then when you see a beautiful sunset, or hear a song, or see a program you are really crying for all the things inside, only those around you don't know, so it is all right, and acceptable."

Willow nodded in agreement. "Yes. People don't think of it if you cry then, at least not so much." There was a deep sadness in her voice that Laurel couldn't help but notice. She marvelled at the wisdom of her sister. Since they had come home to Phoenix she was beginning to see the city through Willow's eyes. Willow had a way of cutting straight to the heart of a thing in a few words as she had done just now. Laurel was more aware of the city's air pollution and noise than she had been before. She had never really noticed or been bothered by them but since her trip and with Willow's keen insight, more and more she knew when she left Phoenix permanently it would be with no regrets.

She turned to Willow, lovely in her pale yellow pants outfit that blended so well with Laurel's pastel green and shyly said, "Willow, are there many tears under the surface for you?"

For a moment she didn't think Willow was going to answer, then she spoke in a barely audible voice. "Yes, Laurel."

Laurel's heart sank. She had so wanted Willow to be happy during her stay in Phoenix. Hesitatingly she reached out her hand. "Is there anything you want to tell me about? Is there anything I can do to make you happier?"

Tears filled Willow's eyes. Finally she whispered, as though it cost her a great deal,

"You could answer a question."

"Anything," Laurel promised, her heart racing. Was she going to discover why Willow often carried the look of sadness? Aunt Jane was in the kitchen making orange juice, and they were alone.

With a tremendous effort Willow asked, "Why is it your Vista d'Oro letters are all from Dr. Cliff?" She added brokenly, "Why do you not hear from Peter?"

"Peter?" Laurel was puzzled. "Peter Thompson? Why should I hear from him?"

"You are promised."

Laurel thought she hadn't heard Willow right. "Promised? Yes, Willow, I am promised, but to Dr. Cliff, not to Peter." Her eyes widened. "Willow! You thought . . . ?" Her voice trailed off.

"I saw you the last night," Willow confessed. "I didn't mean to pry, but you were standing in front of the chapel and then . . ."

Laurel grabbed her in a tight embrace.

"I had just told him of my love for Dr. Cliff. He was so happy he kissed me!" Willow dropped her head in shame while her heart beat wildly. Then Peter didn't care for Laurel, except as a sister! A great gladness filled her.

Laurel saw the look and understood. All these weeks she had thought Peter loved her

208

twin, Willow had hidden it. This was the reason for her sadness. Now pure joy shone in her face.

"You just gave me the most wonderful Christmas present in the whole world," she told Laurel, who was tongue-tied with emotion. The words tumbled out, how she had not been asleep in the car on the way to Flagstaff, how she had overheard Laurel tell Aunt Jane of her plans, all the time thinking it was Peter she was planning to marry.

"Dr. Cliff! He is wonderful. I can see now how you felt."

Laurel was stricken with remorse. "I should have told you," she exclaimed. "But Dr. Cliff was so insistent I come home for a few months and we were afraid you wouldn't come if you knew the truth, for fear you were keeping me from him. I never dreamed you were worrying about Peter." Quickly she made her decision. She told Willow how at the very last moment Peter had been going to confess his love, but on that fateful Thanksgiving evening, it had turned out to be the wrong girl.

"He really loves me?" Willow couldn't believe her own ears, yet her heart was stoutly confirming the truth of her sister's words. "Then I will go back to Vista d'Oro too." She went on to tell Laurel how she had planned to stay in Phoenix but how after she came, although it fascinated her, she dreaded living anywhere except Vista d'Oro. Laurel was shocked at the burden her sister had carried.

Their confessions were interrupted by Aunt Jane and tall glasses of orange juice. At Willow's nod of permission, Laurel told her the whole story.

"Land sakes, Willow, why didn't you ask me?" Aunt Jane wanted to know.

"I didn't know there was anything to question," she replied, and only then did Laurel and Aunt Jane realize the strain she had been under.

The logs in the fireplace had burned low before they got to bed that night, but each of them drifted off to sleep enfolded in happiness. Aunt Jane knew now they would all be going back to Vista d'Oro in the spring. "And live happily ever after," she said to herself with a grin. Laurel rejoiced in her sister's look as they had said good night. And Willow slept like a child. Her troubles were over.

Chapter 13

The days following Christmas Eve sped by. There was a completely different atmosphere in the O'Hara household that stemmed from Willow's learning the truth about Laurel and Peter Thompson. She sang as she helped about the place and one day approached Laurel with a new idea.

"Is there any way I could learn some simple facts of nursing while I'm here? I'm well and strong now, and if I could take some kind of course before spring comes it would really help in Vista d'Oro." She blushed. "I don't mean a whole training course for LPN or RN like you and Mrs. Molly. If what you say of Peter is true, I don't want to stay away a whole year! But isn't there something I could do?"

Laurel was excited at the plan. "Give me some time to do some checking," she said. "I'll find out what's available."

Within a few days everything was set. Laurel had talked with her supervisor, Mrs. Murray, explaining the whole situation. Mrs. Murray listened carefully, taking note of the fact Willow had already some limited experience working in the clinic.

She told Laurel, "I think if Willow wanted to we could find a place for her right here in Ward Four. I've wanted a good aide to help your friend Beth Duncan with the children, especially those recovering from surgery or broken bones. It's hard for those active youngsters to stay down. Would she like that? She could also do some observing in other parts of the hospital on her time off."

She looked curiously at Laurel. "Will it bother you having her here?"

"Bother me?" Laurel was indignant. "She's my sister!"

Mrs. Murray smiled quietly. She was glad Laurel reacted that way. There would be the usual flareup of gossip, but in a few days the staff would be too busy to care about Willow's relationship to Laurel.

It was arranged that Willow would come in with Beth, whose home was fairly close to the O'Hara residence, and ride home with Laurel, whose shift overlapped Beth's. This would give her four hours in Ward 4 and two hours for temporary assignments to other areas of the hospital. The first morning she was too excited to eat. Her dark hair was neatly caught back with a clasp and her yellow aide's uniform set off her coloring. She could hardly wait! And to think she would be working with the children and on Laurel's own ward! She had never dreamed it would be possible.

Within a few days, as soon as she had learned where things were, Willow had made herself invaluable. Never had Beth seen such a willing aide. No task was too menial, no child too fussy to dent the calmness of her new helper. Beth's large gray eyes took in everything, and Willow was drawn to her from the first, as Laurel had been. Sometimes they would have a few minutes' break at the same time, and little by little Willow revealed her past life to Beth. It was a good thing Willow's uniform was yellow, Laurel's white, or the whole ward would have been in confusion. Mrs. Murray sighed when she saw them, knowing it was only a matter of time until she would lose them both. Although neither girl had said anything to her about leaving in the spring, she knew they were too beautiful not to be snatched up by eager admirers.

So January with its long days and February slowly passed. On Valentine's Day when the girls arrived home Aunt Jane was in a dither. Two florist's boxes had arrived, one for Laurel, a smaller one for Willow.

Wonderingly, Willow watched Laurel open hers first. Willow had never received flowers before. "Oh," Laurel breathed as she gently took the waxy green paper aside and brought out a dozen red roses.

"Sweetheart roses," Aunt Jane put in, a twinkle in her eye. Laurel blushed then read the tiny card. "Spring will come — your Cliff."

"Open yours, Willow," Aunt Jane urged. Slowly the girl opened the box. Inside was an old-fashioned bouquet. One pink rose was in the center, surrounded by small blue flowers that brought a sparkle to Willow's eyes. She knew what those tiny blue flowers were — forget-me-nots. The card was simply signed "Peter."

The girls couldn't know it had been Mrs. Molly who instigated the floral offering. Dr. Cliff had to make a trip to Flagstaff and she had told him, "Why don't you send your girl some posies?"

Dr. Cliff's eyes gleamed. "Maybe I will," he said casually, then he turned to Peter.

"How about it, Peter? Shall I send a little something from you to Willow, just to let her know you're glad she's so much better?"

Peter thought for a moment, then said, "Yes, why don't you?" Mrs. Molly had done the rest. She took Dr. Cliff aside and told him, "When you send the flowers from Peter, tell them to throw in a handful of for-get-me-nots."

Both Dr. Cliff and Peter had spent a lot of time with Mrs. Molly that winter. Accidents were few and for once business at the clinic wasn't at quite such a breakneck pace. They had worked on the clinic cottage until it was cosy and bright. Mrs. Molly had also casually suggested that as long as they were in the mood, they might as well fix up Peter's place a bit too. He hadn't seemed to care too much one way or the other, but she took his nod for a go-ahead, and by Valentine's Day the small house by the chapel was also very comfortable.

Peter lived for Laurel's letters almost as much as Dr. Cliff and Mrs. Molly did. She was wonderful about writing, and always included special parts for her doctor to share with the others. She stressed the way Willow was improving and told them they wouldn't know her when spring came. She told how Willow loved working with the children, yet how so often now she would come upon her standing by a window, gazing north.

Laurel also shyly confessed how more and more she was anxious to leave the city behind. "It's been a wonderful winter," she closed one letter, "but I feel that life is just really about to begin for me — and for Willow and Aunt Jane." She didn't add that Christmas Eve she had given away Peter's secret. In time he would know and forgive her.

It had been decided that the girls and Aunt Jane wouldn't go back to Vista d'Oro until the first of May. They had wanted to go in April, but Desert General had finally been able to plan the memorial service for Dr. O'Hara and wanted it in late April. They insisted Laurel must be present to say a few words or the occasion would be spoiled. Out of respect to those who had loved her father so much Laurel finally agreed.

In the meantime, as soon as the weather permitted the three of them were making short trips. The girls worked several days in a row, then had a few extra hours off and they put them to good use. Willow marvelled at Oak Creek Canyon and the South Rim even more than Laurel had done so many months ago. She stood transfixed on the spot where Laurel had rescued the small boy, cheeks pale at what could have happened.

They had hoped the doctor and Peter could get away and meet them at Flagstaff or the South Rim, but a minor epidemic of colds and flu had hit Vista d'Oro and they couldn't leave. Peter was pressed into service at the clinic in whatever way he could help, and Dr. Cliff and Mrs. Molly were run ragged. It was all Aunt Jane could do to keep the girls from dropping everything and going to help, but at last she convinced them it was the way Dr. Cliff and Peter wanted it, and they reluctantly had to agree.

While Mrs. Molly was refurnishing and sprucing up Dr. Cliff and Peter's homes, Aunt Jane was having the time of her life in Phoenix. Once it had been determined they were all three going back to Vista d'Oro, she got a wild scheme in her head. It wouldn't be too long, she was sure, before Willow would no longer need Mrs. Molly's extra bedroom, so one day without saying anything to the girls Aunt Jane wrote and asked Mrs. Molly if she would like to have her live with her. She could use the couch until Willow was married.

The answer came by return mail. She was more than welcome. A grin quirked her lips as she answered it. Would Mrs. Molly send her the room dimensions? She had some furniture of her own she would like to bring if it was all right.

When she got the information she chuckled and proceeded to make many mysterious shopping trips while the girls were both away. They were totally unsuspecting of the various packages and orders

Aunt Jane had been tucking away. She had determined to do something for Mrs. Molly, who did so very much for others. She took part of her savings and went on a spree that brought a dent to her bank account but a glow of pride to her heart. Now she could hardly wait for May to come! In the meantime she was also doing shopping for Laurel, sheets and towels, blankets and pillowcases. It was a pleasure to pick out the beautiful linen for the big cedar chest Laurel had bought.

Laurel had her hands full those days. In addition to her work, she was doing personal shopping for a trousseau for herself and without Willow's knowing it, a separate one for her! It would be her wedding gift. Laurel had a feeling when Peter and Willow settled things he wasn't going to wait for her to assemble a trousseau. She smiled at the thought. Her surprise would be very welcome. She had also instructed Aunt Jane to buy equal numbers of all the items in her own hope chest and store them in a spare closet back out of sight. Laurel wanted her sister to start out with everything she herself would have.

At last the day came for the girls to shop for Laurel's wedding dress. She searched and searched before finding just the right gown, white lace, floor-length but without a train. She chose a simple Juliet pearl beaded cap instead of a veil.

"I don't want to show off," she told Willow. "We have definitely decided to be married in Peter's chapel. I think the village will enjoy that."

Willow looked at her beautiful sister in her bridal white without a trace of envy. "If Peter and I ever get married, would you let me wear your dress?"

Laurel looked at her sister quickly. "Wouldn't you want your own?"

"I'd rather borrow yours," Willow told her, sincerity in every word.

Laurel only smiled. Only too well did she know Willow would be wearing the dress probably much sooner than she thought! Carefully she removed the gown and had it packed away in a satin-lined box. It was perfect. She wouldn't have to do anything except press it when her wedding day came.

"Now we must get dresses for the memorial service," she told Willow. When her sister protested she didn't need anything new, Laurel said, "Willow, this may be the only time Dad's friends ever get to see his other daughter. He would want you to have the best." Willow said no more except to tell

Laurel she would have to make the final selection.

At last in a small shop they found just what Laurel wanted. Sapphire-blue velvet gowns, identical, floor length yet simple. The softest velvet imaginable.

"We can use them for hostess gowns when we have our 'high teas' in Vista d'Oro," she whispered to Willow, who giggled outright. They were lovely and when the two girls were dressed, Aunt Jane couldn't contain herself.

"If you fix your hair the same for the memorial service no one will be able to tell you apart!" A glint of mischief crossed her face, then she added teasingly, "Willow can give your speech, Laurel."

Willow's eyes grew wide with alarm and she shook her head. "Not me! I'm going to sit in the back row."

Laurel didn't tell her it had been arranged ahead of time she would be sitting in the front row. Laurel had a special reason for doing this, but now was not the time to reveal it.

It seemed now there weren't enough hours in the day to get everything done. One weekend they dropped everything and traveled back to the little white church in Globe, receiving the same warm welcome as before. Laurel had wanted to go on into the White Mountains but it was too early. They might just get snowbound.

"Someday," she promised Willow. "Someday we'll find time for it."

In Vista d'Oro things were happening too. Peter had been delighted with the thank-you note for Willow's Valentine bouquet, although slightly mystified at one sentence:

". . . . the small blue flowers were especially beautiful."

Seeking out Dr. Cliff he demanded, "Just what kind of flowers were in that bouquet you sent Willow from me?"

Dr. Cliff laughed aloud. "A pink rose, some white doodabs, and a handful of little blue flowers."

Peter's eyes never wavered. "What kind of little blue flowers?"

Dr. Cliff had the grace to look ashamed. "Well, I think Mrs. Molly said to ask for forget-me-nots." He threw up his hands in mock fright. "Don't blame me, it was all Mrs. Molly's idea."

Peter's grin spread across his whole face. "It's probably the best thing you ever did for me." He went out whistling, leaving Dr. Cliff to look after him amazed. He had been afraid Peter would be angry. Instead he had evidently done him a favor! Not knowing of

Willow's thank you, he just didn't understand Peter's attitude.

As the months had progressed Peter began to wonder if he was really doing the right thing. According to everything he could learn from Laurel and Aunt Jane's letters, plus what Mrs. Molly told him, the last thing Willow wanted to do was be away from Vista d'Oro any longer than necessary. Her longing for home struck a responsive chord in him, and as he went about his duties his stern decision to hold back his offer of love from her began to fade. At last on a beautiful April day he climbed the "O'Hare mesa," as he and Dr. Cliff jokingly nicknamed it, and sat down under the great pinyon tree that had seen so many troubles.

Lifting his face to the sky he earnestly prayed, "Am I wrong? Do I have the right to tell her I care?" The peace of the spring sunshine seemed to persuade him, and with it came a feeling of rightness. He knew Willow would be a helpmate for him in his work, and he rejoiced. Casting another look at the beautiful sunlit village he hurried down the trail, yet being careful not to slip. He had not yet completely conquered the anger he felt when he thought of Dr. Carson and how he had caused Willow's fall that day.

When the clinic closed that evening Peter

sauntered in. "May I use your phone?" he asked. There was nothing to indicate anything unusual in the request. He often used the phone to Flagstaff, always keeping track of the charges so he could reimburse the clinic. This time, however, he closed the door behind him. Dr. Cliff's eyebrows raised, but he felt whatever Peter wanted him to know he would share later so asked no questions.

Peter got the number and rang the O'Hara residence, but Aunt Jane was the only one home. Both of the girls had been asked by Beth Duncan to have dinner with her. It would be late before they got home. "Can I take a message?" she asked.

Peter was frustrated by not being able to get hold of Willow now he had made up his mind. "Yes," he shouted into the phone, unlike the usually reserved Peter Aunt Jane knew. "Tell Willow I love her and if she will spend the rest of her life in Vista d'Oro, I want to marry her! I will be gone the next few days so she can't call but have her send a telegram so it will be here when I get back." He paused for breath and Aunt Jane put in a word before he could go on:

"Yes, sir!"

"I'm sorry, Aunt Jane," he apologized. "It's just that I've finally felt free to speak and now I want her to know before all those Phoenix guys that must be after her make too big of an impression." Aunt Jane didn't tell him neither Willow nor Laurel had gone out on dates since their return from Vista d'Oro. She was smiling as she hung up the phone and carefully wrote his message, word for word, and pinned it to Willow's pillow, leaving her bedlight on so she would be sure to see it.

When Willow read the note she laughed, then cried, then laughed some more. How like Peter! Once he had decided he wasn't wasting any time, that was for sure. How should she answer it? She didn't want to send a mushy telegram. Somehow she felt their love was too precious even to share with a teletype operator. Then she had it. Peter was a missionary, he would understand.

Calling Western Union, she said in a trembling voice, "I would like to send a telegram to Mr. Peter Thompson, Vista d'Oro, Arizona. The message is Ruth sixteen."

"Ruth sixteen? Is that all?" the perplexed operator asked.

"Yes," Willow replied firmly. "And sign it Willow." Hanging up the telephone and preparing for bed, she could visualize Peter's face when he received the message. She had once heard him preach on what seemed to her among the most beautiful words she had ever heard: "Entreat me not to leave thee, or to return from following after thee; for whither thou goest I will go; and where thou lodgest, I will lodge; thy people shall be my people, and thy God my God." Peter would have his answer, and would treasure the way she had chosen to give it.

Chapter 14

The auditorium was brilliantly lighted. Even Laurel had never seen it so beautifully decorated. There were flags against the white walls, and streamers of red, white, and blue crepe paper made a background for the speakers. She whispered to Willow, "We certainly chose our gowns well. We look like part of the decorations!"

Willow smiled appreciatively. "I didn't realize how many people respected our father." She was different tonight, the beautiful sapphire-blue gown had added self-confidence. Aunt Jane had urged them to wear their hair alike, so they had found bands of the same dress velvet and swept their dark locks back in shining falls, slightly turned under at the ends. Even Aunt Jane called Laurel "Willow" once!

"Right down here." Laurel guided Willow and Aunt Jane to the front seats in front of the speaker's stand. Head high, but with heart beating rapidly, Willow and Aunt Jane took their places and watched Laurel go to the chairman for final instructions.

In a matter of minutes Laurel, the chief of the hospital staff, and the chairman of the

Board of Directors were seated on the platform in front of the microphones. Willow marvelled at the composure with which Laurel could sit there laughing and talking in a low tone with the two men. Pride swelled inside her to be part of Laurel, and part of this, she added, looking around the big room. It seemed half of Desert General plus others had come!

At last the ceremony started. The national anthem was sung, a short invocation was given, then the chairman of the Board spoke. He spoke of the tradition Desert General had, its goal one of dedicated service to those who came within its doors. He spoke of Dr. O'Hara and the many years of service he had given.

"We all owe the memory of this man a great deal," he stated soberly. There was a spontaneous burst of applause when he finished.

The chief of staff was next. He told several amusing and inspirational incidents from Dr. O'Hara's years at the hospital. He spoke in a way that made the big redheaded doctor seem alive and present with them, and others besides the two girls had wet eyes when he closed with:

"Dr. O'Hara is part of the proud heritage of those who have literally given their lives in the service of others. We honor and respect him for it." He searched the audience intently, then added, "We are extremely fortunate to have his charming daughter here tonight to speak a word. We also feel it fitting at the end of tonight's service to announce Dr. O'Hara's successor." A ripple of anticipation swept the audience. In the third row Debi Thorne Carson clutched her husband's sleeve, eyes shining. Dr. Carson sat up a little straighter, a satisfied look on his face. He was proud of Debi tonight — she was beautiful in her sea-green gown, red hair carefully dressed in the latest style. He himself wore an expensive tailored suit. He felt they should look their best when the presentation was made.

As Laurel stood and crossed to the microphone an involuntary clapping started, a tribute not only for Dr. O'Hara, but for his beautiful daughter standing there in her sapphire gown. It continued until she raised her hand for silence and began to speak.

"I will never be able to thank you enough for this service. I recognize it as love for my father. You spoke well" — she smiled at the chief of staff — "when you said my father had left a proud heritage for us. No one knows this better than I. My father was one in a million. Even his death from overwork in the service of others proved that." She brushed back a tear.

"But this is not a time for sad memories. This is a time for joy." Pausing for a moment, she took a deep breath, then spoke again.

"I have another heritage in addition to that of my father. It is also a very proud one. I only learned of it recently — even my father did not know all about it." In a torrent of words, each enunciated clearly, she held her audience spellbound as she told of how Dr. O'Hara had met and loved Cloudy Willow. She told the whole story frankly, of her father's dream to spend his life with the Navajo people, of his shattered world when he lost his beautiful Indian wife. There wasn't a sound in the audience, they were too caught up in her story.

Dr. Grant Carson leaned back in his seat, a complacent smile on his face. What a fool she was! To stand up there and announce her mixture of race! It was a good thing he had married Debi. Tonight's performance would have killed any hope he had of being Dr. O'Hara's successor.

When Laurel finished her story she gazed straight into her sister's eyes. Leaving the platform she went down the steps to the front row, took Willow's hand, and led her to the microphone.

"This is my sister, Willow," she told them simply. "My father couldn't fulfill his dream, but we are going back to Vista d'Oro." A rich blush mantled her smooth cheek. "I am to marry Dr. Clifford Barclay, and Willow is to marry Peter Thompson, a missionary. We plan to spend the rest of our lives in the service of our people."

No one ever knew afterward who started the cheering. Some said it was Debi Carson. At least she was one of the first on her feet in a standing ovation for the two girls on the platform, typifying the best of two American races, Irish and Navajo. In spite of Grant's trying to make her sit down she persisted.

"They deserve it," she told him sharply, the glint of battle in her eye. "You'd better get up, you're conspicuous by your being seated."

It was true. The entire group was on their feet, cheering and clapping.

In one corner Mrs. Murray sighed to Beth Duncan. "I knew I'd lose them, but you know? I can't be sorry. They're needed more there than at Mountainside. Vista d'Oro, what a lovely name!"

"Yes," Beth agreed, her hands sore from applauding. "And those two girls will be totally happy there."

When the chief of staff finally raised his big hand for silence and the shuffle of chairs ceased, he turned to the two girls standing side by side.

"Willow, would you like to say anything to these friends of your father and Laurel, and now you?" He didn't really expect her to speak — he had noticed her shyness as she came forward with Laurel. To his amazement and even more so to Laurel's, Willow tremblingly stepped to the microphone.

"It is hard for me to speak," she faltered. "But I could not leave your city without telling you something. When I came to Phoenix I was afraid, even with my sister. The white people have not always been kind to my people." She glanced imperceptibly at Dr. Carson, then back to Aunt Jane, whose big smile encouraged her.

"You have welcomed me. I have worked at Mountainside. I have been in some of your homes. I have been treated as a royal guest. I must thank you. When I go home to Vista d'Oro" — she pressed a hand to her heart — "part of me will be here with my father's people."

The applause was thunderous. The audience sensed how hard it had been for her to stand, yet how she had felt she must do this for them. Tears flowed freely down Laurel's beautiful cheeks and she hugged her sister, pride evident in her face.

In the back of the room two men looked deep into each other's eyes. Each was thinking the same. This was the first time Dr. O'Hara and Peter had seen Laurel and Willow in their Phoenix setting, gowned in clothing other than uniform, traditional Navajo garb for Willow, or pants outfits for Laurel. The thought crossed each mind, reflected in the other's eyes. They were glad they had secured the girls' promise of marriage before tonight! There was something so regal about the two girls in their expensive gowns that they seemed a little unapproachable. It was almost beyond belief that they would not be willing, but anxious to return to Vista d'Oro! But they had made it clear to all, not knowing their fiances were present, what their intentions were.

When the girls were seated again, another chair hastily provided for Willow to be beside her sister, the chief of staff again took the stand.

"There has been much speculation about who would be selected to follow Dr. O'Hara as Chief Surgeon of Desert General. I won't say 'fill his shoes' for it will be a long time before that can happen." An appreciative

232

chuckle rippled through the listeners.

"A lot of consideration has been given to several worthy doctors," he went on, eyes sweeping the audience until at last they rested a little longer on Dr. Carson than the others.

"Many factors have been taken into consideration, and at last our decision has been reached. The doctor chosen is one of professional integrity beyond reproach. He is also one of the finest men I have ever known."

Dr. Carson's face glowed. To have a tribute from the chief of staff even before he was announced! What a plum! For a moment he was lost in a daydream from which determination grew. He would pull every string, use every bit of influence and someday he would replace the man who now stood before them. He would become chief of staff!

Dr. Carson was so lost in his own thoughts that when the chief of staff announced, "I think Dr. O'Hara himself would have selected this doctor if he could have chosen his replacement. I give you Dr. Alan McIntosh!" he started to rise.

"What are you doing?" Debi hissed, jerking him back in his seat. "It isn't you!" Her voice had the effect of an ice-cold shower. He glared at her.

"It has to be!"

"Well, it isn't!" she snapped. "Now applaud and smile. At least show a little sportsmanship." Dr. Carson managed to paste a phony smile on his face and clap a few times, but inside he was burning! What a glaring error he had made! It was all Laurel's fault! If she hadn't given that emotional speech none of those present would have been swayed to accept her heritage.

"Let's get out of here," he muttered, dragging Debi toward the door, but her temper was rising.

"We're going up front, stand in line with the others and congratulate Dr. McIntosh!" Her voice softened a bit at the stricken look in Grant's eyes. "It's the only way. There will be other jobs, and if you act like a spoiled child about this one it will kill any future chances!"

Gritting his teeth, Dr. Carson had to admit the logic of her words. He managed to say a few words to the new Chief Surgeon, smile and speak to Laurel and murmur, "It's nice to see you again, Willow," before melting into the crowd. Debi's handshake was firm, and Laurel could see sincerity in her eyes for the first time. She realized now that Debi had really loved Dr. Carson — her maliciousness was born of that love. Graciously she smiled, and the warmth went straight to Debi's heart. Debi felt a queer kind of choking envy as she turned away. Yes, Debi had married Grant Carson, but she knew it would not bring the happiness that shone in Laurel's eyes. Laurel watched her go, compassion in her gaze. Yet even as Debi was lost from sight she thought, I think she can make a success. That red hair and temper will keep him in line as much as anyone ever could!

It wasn't until the well-wishers had thinned down to a very few that Willow glanced up, her gaze transfixed. "Look!" She pointed with a trembling finger. Down the aisle, side by side as though marching to the sound of drums, came Dr. Cliff and Peter! There was a look in their faces that instantly reappeared in the girls' eyes and like homing pigeons they flew to their men. Amid tears and laughter Laurel noticed the broad grin Aunt Jane had been trying to hide.

"You knew all the time!" she accused, but there was only joy in her voice.

Aunt Jane brushed off her accusation. "Don't you think I picked well?" she asked the unexpected visitors, motioning to the girls' corsages against the glowing blue.

When the doctor and Peter found they could get away they had phoned Aunt Jane and told her to select flowers. They would arrive too late to present them in person. Secretly she had ordered exact replicas of the Valentine bouquets. Laurel's was a corsage of red sweetheart roses against silver ribbon, Willow's was a single pink rose, surrounded by white and tiny blue forget-me-nots!

It was arranged that Peter would take Willow and drive Laurel's white Mustang home. Dr. Cliff would take Laurel and Aunt Jane in his car.

When Willow was seated beside Peter he made no move to start the car. Instead he looked at her, "Willow, did you really mean your message?" The look in her eyes was answer enough. He gathered her close for their first embrace. Then still holding her he asked, "When will you marry me?"

"Whenever you like," she said simply.

"Tomorrow?"

She gasped at his question but only said, "Yes, Peter," never once thinking how it could be accomplished.

Peter went on to explain that his mission board had given him a two-week vacation if he took it then. "We could have a honeymoon anywhere you like," he went on. "Laurel and Dr. Cliff said they wanted to wait until about mid-May so the North Rim would be open for their honeymoon. Also, he has a friend, an older man who is tired from overwork in his Salt Lake City hospital and has offered to stay at the clinic while they are gone. This way we could be back in plenty of time for the wedding in Vista d'Oro."

Willow whispered shyly, "I would like to take you to Oak Creek Canyon and back to the South Rim." Peter thought it was a great idea. So did Dr. Cliff and Laurel, when they discussed it with them. "Good thing you just *happened* to pick up a marriage license on the way down," he teased.

"Oh!" Willow had never thought of that. Then another thought hit her. Following Laurel into the kitchen, she whispered, "But I have no white dress! What should I do?"

"You'll wear the one in the closet," Laurel replied calmly.

Willow's eyes opened wider. "But that is yours! I was going to borrow it *after* you were married!"

Laurel's smile was tender. "What difference does it make? We're twins, aren't we?"

So it was settled. The only problem was that they didn't know a church in Phoenix where either Willow or Laurel knew the pastor.

Hesitant to seem too managing, Laurel tentatively asked, "Would you want to be married in that little white chapel in Globe, Willow?"

Willow's face brightened. "Do you think it could be arranged?" She looked to Peter for confirmation.

"That would be fine with me," he agreed heartily. He didn't care where they were married, as long as it was soon!

"Then we could start our honeymoon trip through the White Mountains where Laurel once traveled," he added, seeing the delight in Willow's face. "What was the name of that little motel?"

Laurel laughed, glad to see how happy Willow and Peter were!

"Pinyon Village," she said. "And the people are Tom and Carol Parker." She dashed to the phone and called the minister of the Globe church. "He says he can marry you at one o'clock tomorrow afternoon," she told them excitedly. "That will be perfect timewise for getting to Pinyon Village."

Willow was so dazed and happy by it all she wasn't much use in getting ready. Finally Laurel told her, "Go amuse Peter! Aunt Jane and I can pack for you." She didn't tell Willow about the complete trousseau she would find when she opened her suitcases.

Aunt Jane was having the time of her life. She too had some surprises that would be coming to light in the future. For now she was busy getting Willow ready.

At one o'clock the next afternoon Willow and Peter stood before the kindly white-haired minister in the little church. Rays of sunlight streamed through the stained glass windows, filling the chapel with color, lightly resting on the lovely bride, touching gently the blue gown of Laurel, who stood with her sister. The words he spoke were solemn, he quoted from Ruth 16:

". . . whither thou goest . . . thy people, my people . . . thy God, my God." Willow and Peter looked at one another in complete happiness. The words were so fitting.

Later would come the tender questions. No, she hadn't told the minister, she hadn't told anyone of her message to him. Much later would come reports of the honeymoon, the delight of the Parkers to meet Laurel's sister, the wonderful closeness of Peter and Willow as they followed the path Aunt Jane had led Laurel on last fall. The spring loveliness of Zane Grey's cabin, Oak Creek, and finally the South Rim. At the moment the minister's closing benediction, "I pronounce you husband and wife. God bless you both throughout your lives," was all that mattered. Dr. Cliff and Laurel were almost as touched by the service as the bridal pair, and even peppery Aunt Jane hid a tear. She was so full she almost burst. The only drop of sadness was that Mrs. Molly hadn't been there.

"She understood," Peter told them. "I told her what I wanted to do if Willow would consent. She said she would make up for it at Laurel's wedding!"

After they waved good-bye to Peter and Willow, the three hastened back to Phoenix. Dr. Cliff had to go back the next day, and it was decided Laurel would accompany him. She demurred at first. There was too much to do. How could she just up and go, with all there was to do?

"Go on," Aunt Jane told her. "I'll take all the time I need and get things ready. We'll have professional movers do most of it. Leave it to me." She set her lips sternly.

"All right," Laurel consented. "It's a good thing the house is already sold." She had had a good offer through the family lawyer, and all the papers had been signed just a few days before.

The drive to Vista d'Oro was wonderful. Spring flowers were everywhere, a carpet of them only about a half inch high. Dr. Cliff told Laurel how the seeds lay under the soil dormant for sometimes many years and when a good spring rain came they all came up and bloomed.

"Like us," she whispered. He needed no explanation. He too felt their love had bloomed from the desert background it had been given many years ago by Dr. O'Hara and Cloudy Willow, and he rejoiced.

Chapter 15

It was late afternoon when Dr. Cliff and Laurel reached Vista d'Oro. Mrs. Molly saw them drive up and rushed to the gate to meet them, her face aglow with excitement.

"Come right in," she welcomed. "I hope you didn't stop for supper. There's a big stew on the stove and it won't take a minute to pop some biscuits in the oven."

Talking a mile a minute, she wanted to know all about Willow and Peter, and Aunt Jane, and the wedding until at last Dr. Cliff said, "Mrs. Molly, give us a chance to breathe!"

She laughed and then was off with another barrage of questions ending with, "And wait until you see!" She led the way into her living room and there were boxes and boxes, addressed to her.

"At first I tried to tell the man there was some mistake," Mrs. Molly said, "but there was my name, plain as the nose on your face." She gestured. "I was afraid to open them so decided to wait until you got here."

Together they carefully opened the shipping crates. There were items ranging from drapes to a small piano. There was a small sewing machine, appliances of every kind. And tucked in the bottom of the smallest box was a little card, "from Aunt Jane."

"I can't accept all this," Mrs. Molly gasped, surrounded by Aunt Jane's thoughtfulness.

"You can't refuse to accept it," Laurel told her. "It would break Aunt Jane's heart if you even mentioned it being too much. She evidently spent a lot of time and thought on these things for your home, which will also be hers. Don't spoil it by refusing. No," she added, "I didn't know anything about it, neither did Willow, I'm sure. Just be glad for such a friend."

"I agree," Dr. Cliff chimed in. "Let her do what she wants." He chuckled. "Sometimes it's harder to be a gracious receiver than a giver!"

A few days later his words came back to him. A great shipment of much-needed equipment arrived at the clinic. "But how?" he asked puzzled, then caught sight of Laurel's laughing face.

"You didn't . . ." he began but she interrupted.

"Sometimes it's harder to be a gracious receiver than a giver!"

He had to laugh in return and capitulated. "How did you know what we most needed?"

"There's always Mrs. Molly," she teased. Growing serious, she told him, "This is Willow's and my wedding present to you. We decided that our father would want it this way. The rest of his savings, and the money from the sale of the house is divided equally between Willow and myself. It isn't a lot, but it can be a backlog in case it is ever needed." A lovely light filled her eyes.

"Perhaps there will be children who will need education . . ." Her remark was too much for Dr. Cliff, and he couldn't help but kiss her then and there.

"Payment on account," he told her.

In a surprisingly short time Aunt Jane and the rest of the furniture and household goods arrived. What a time they had fitting everything into the three homes! The clinic cottage housed some of the O'Hara furniture, but much of it went into Peter's little home by the chapel. Thanks to Aunt Jane, before Peter and Willow arrived, glowing from their honeymoon, everything was in perfect order. She had not only taken over the cooking for overnight clinic patients, she kept Dr. Cliff and Laurel and Mrs. Molly supplied with fresh-baked bread and good food.

"My way of helping the clinic," she told them tartly, although pleased at their praise.

"I can't patch people up, but I can feed them!"

A few days after Peter and Willow came home another person arrived in Vista d'Oro, Dr. James Mackenzie. He was in his early fifties, a big man, although the strain of his work had left him rather thin and tired-looking. He was Aunt Jane's special project.

"Hmph! If I can't fatten him up a bit while he's here my name isn't Jane Scott," she told Laurel. Laurel's eyes twinkled.

"Better not spoil him too much. His wife died several years ago, and I overheard him telling Cliff he hadn't seen such a good homemaker since until he ate your cooking!"

"Go on," Aunt Jane told her snappily, but after Laurel had gone said to herself, "So he thinks I'm a good homemaker," and blushed at the idea.

May 15 was the date Dr. Cliff and Laurel had set for their wedding. It was to be in the morning in Peter's little chapel, with a feast for the village afterward. Everyone in town rejoiced at Dr. O'Hara's other daughter coming to live among them. Gone was all jealousy toward Willow now that she was safely married, and it was to be an occasion for everyone, even the children.

Peter and Willow had decorated the chapel, using the means at hand from the desert.

"She would want it that way," Willow said when Peter suggested ordering flowers from Flagstaff. So when Laurel walked down the aisle of the little chapel on Dr. Mackenzie's arm, it would be among sweet-smelling desert growth, but she would carry red sweetheart roses, Dr. Cliff had seen to that!

The days seemed to rush by. Laurel had insisted on working right up until the time they were to leave.

"Between Mrs. Molly, Willow, and Aunt Jane, they haven't left me anything to do except get dressed on our wedding day," she told Dr. Cliff. "So I might as well be working."

Dr. Mackenzie eyed her curiously. He had wondered how a Phoenix beauty would adapt to this simple village. He found she was part of it from the time he first met her.

Dr. Mackenzie had some strange feelings within himself these days. He felt better out here in the desert than he had felt for years. Although he worked even harder, much of it was outdoors. He rode the jeep or battered station wagon with Dr. Cliff and Peter, marveling at the comfort they brought, espe-

246

cially to those living in the outer edges of the mesa country. He couldn't help but see how needed more help was, and began to wonder. Was it really worth it knocking himself out in a city? There were other capable doctors there, and many nurses.

Here there was only Dr. Cliff, Laurel, Willow, and Mrs. Molly. A pleased look came into his eyes. He had almost forgotten to add Aunt Jane. Without her, Vista d'Oro wouldn't be the same, he admitted to himself. She was a wonderful woman. He had promised to stay until the middle of June, and when he got back to Salt Lake City, he had some tall thinking to do. He smiled to himself. Maybe they would all be seeing him again sooner than they thought! In the meantime, there would be plenty to do while Dr. Cliff and Laurel were away.

Never had a day dawned brighter than Laurel's wedding day. Afterward there would only be a blur of memories. Willow, bridesmaid in her beautiful blue velvet. The village children oohing and ahing at the white lace gown. Tears in Mrs. Molly's eyes. The firm grip of Dr. Mackenzie's hand before they started down the aisle. Aunt Jane's gaze resting approvingly on her, then admiringly at Dr. Mackenzie in his dark suit. Laurel barely suppressed a giggle —

Aunt Jane was probably beaming with pride at the way she had helped Dr. Mackenzie get some meat on his bones!

She quickly sobered as she met Dr. Cliff's eyes and took his hand. Peter's words were clear, beautiful. He had chosen to again use Ruth 16 and had asked Laurel to memorize it. When they took their vows she repeated, her voice clear, her eyes steady on Dr. Cliff's:

"Entreat me not to leave thee, or to return from following after thee; for whither thou goest I will go; and where thou lodgest, I will lodge; thy people shall be my people, and thy God my God."

Dr. Cliff's grip on her hand was strong and tender, and she caught herself thinking as he pledged to love and cherish her in sickness and health, as long as they both should live, he will always be this way. Strong and tender. A deeper love than she had ever felt for him before welled up inside her, and her heart and soul spoke wedding promises far greater than the words.

One of the moments from her wedding day that Laurel would remember was when the chief of the tribe came to her at the feast. A little pool of silence formed when he stepped to where she and Willow stood together for a moment.

Solemnly he said, "Bow your head." Laurel felt something slide over her hair and she opened her eyes. The chief had placed a hand-wrought necklace of silver and turquoise around her neck. It was intricately carved, showing painstaking work. Her blue eyes looked into the chief's dark ones.

"Thank you." It was all she could say.

Turning to Willow, the chief again said, "Bow your head," and placed an identical necklace around her neck. It was a beautiful moment, one neither girl would ever forget. It showed they were totally accepted by the village and would from now on be part of it.

Laurel and Dr. Cliff had planned to leave by mid-afternoon, but the festivities had continued longer than planned. It was nearly sunset when they prepared to leave. Laurel had changed to a dusty pink pantquit and comfortable shoes. Dr. Cliff was casual in his whipcords and blue shirt. No city honeymoon for them!

As they slipped out the door of the clinic cottage, Laurel looked at him longingly, afraid to ask what was in her mind.

Seeing the look, he told her, "We have time to climb O'Hara mesa if you like." Hand in hand they started up the trail to the great pinyon tree.

Peter and Willow saw them go, and hurriedly procured a sign that had been hidden for several days. Making sure they were far enough away not to notice, they took a hammer and nails, and grinning, affixed the sign to the front door of the clinic. They knew the newlyweds would have to pass by it on their way to the white Mustang.

The sunset from the mesa was more glorious than ever before, beyond description. Dr. Cliff and Laurel watched the golden rays touch the land and the same feelings that had touched so many of their days now came.

"View of gold," Laurel whispered, unwilling to break the stillness surrounding them. The sun's rays touched her beautiful face and glorious hair. Dr. Cliff's heart swelled. He drew her closer, content to let his love for her speak for itself.

At last they left their hilltop reluctantly and walked back to the clinic. As they rounded the corner on their way to the Mustang Laurel noticed the sign on the door.

"What's that?" she asked.

Dr. Cliff followed her pointing finger, as mystified as Laurel. Slowly they approached, curious to see what the sign was.

The last ray of the sun illuminated the carved motto, so carefully done, and there before them were the words

O'HARA CLINIC

In memory of Dr. Mike O'Hara
and his beloved wife
Cloudy Willow

Too touched to speak, Laurel stood silently before the tribute, then whispered, "What a heritage for all the years to come! For our children and their children . . . forever."

"Yes," Dr. Cliff said reverently, "and it is a proud heritage."

The sun dropped out of sight, leaving the sign and the clinic in darkness, but as Dr. Cliff and Laurel started toward the Mustang and a new life, the inscription was etched on their hearts with glowing letters. The future lay ahead — they must continue the proud heritage that was theirs.

We hope you have enjoyed this Large Print book. Other Thorndike Press or Chivers Press Large Print books are available at your library or directly from the publishers.

For more information about current and upcoming titles, please call or write, without obligation, to:

Thorndike Press
P.O. Box 159
Thorndike, Maine 04986 USA
Tel. (800) 257-5157

OR

Chivers Press Limited
Windsor Bridge Road
Bath BA2 3AX
England
Tel. (0225) 335336

All our Large Print titles are designed for easy reading, and all our books are made to last.